"It's a good l

"But you have never known anything else," Raul said.

"I've read books. I know something about the way other people live. They aren't necessarily happier than we are."

"No, they aren't," he agreed. "And a lot of them don't have much choice in the way they live, either. But I think your options are unnecessarily limited, Maria. By arranging his life the way he wants it, your father is stopping you from making the most of yours."

Anne Weale was still at school when a women's magazine published some of her stories. At twenty-five, she had her first romance novel accepted. Now, with a grown-up son, and still happily married to her first love, Anne divides her life between her winter home—a Spanish village ringed by mountains and vineyards—and a summer place in Guernsey—one of the many islands around the world she has used as backgrounds for her books.

Books by Anne Weale

HARLEQUIN ROMANCE

HARLEQUIN PRESENTS

TEQUILA SUNRISE
Anne Weale

Harlequin Books

TORONTO • NEW YORK • LONDON
AMSTERDAM • PARIS • SYDNEY • HAMBURG
STOCKHOLM • ATHENS • TOKYO • MILAN
MADRID • WARSAW • BUDAPEST • AUCKLAND

For Adrienne, Bettina, Joan and Margaret
who shared the Yucatan experience.
And especially for Charlotte who, when her dream
holiday turned into a nightmare,
proved herself a real-life heroine.

ISBN 0-373-17240-0

TEQUILA SUNRISE

Copyright © 1994 by Anne Weale.

First North American Publication 1995.

PROLOGUE

As HER taxi left central London, Maria pushed back the sleeve of her shiny black puffa jacket to check the time. Her scheduled flight to Madrid was due to take off from Heathrow airport at five. Would she make it? She must!

It was less than thirty-six hours since she had flown back to London after a strenuous tour of the workshops in south-east Asia where many of her designs were manufactured.

Yesterday, purely by chance, she had read in *The Times* that an exhibition of paintings was opening tonight at Spain's famous Prado Museum in the presence of the American and British ambassadors and of many distinguished members of the international art fraternity, including the owner of the collection, Raul Dysart.

It was seven years since she had last seen him and time was supposed to heal all wounds. But not this one. The injury he had inflicted was as irreparable as an amputation.

At the time there was nothing she could do about it. Except run away and hide. But now it was different. She was no longer a defenceless innocent. She had the means to retaliate. A glittering occasion was the perfect time to do it.

It had been cold in London. In Madrid it was colder. In spite of her down-lined puffa, the razor-edged wind blowing from the surrounding *sierras* made Maria shiver as she hurried into the lobby of her hotel. After growing up in the sun, she had never completely adjusted to European winters.

Many of the top people attending the reception tonight would be staying at the Ritz Hotel, close to the Prado. Certainly Raul would be there, unless he was a guest of the British Embassy. As she didn't want to risk an encounter with him beforehand, she had told her assistant to make a reservation at one of the city's less famous hotels.

She was known in Spain. Both Galerias Preciados and El Corte Inglès, the two big nationwide department stores, stocked her designs, and she had appeared on programmes for women viewers on Spanish TV. Always wearing the large tinted glasses and big-brimmed mannish hats which, at the beginning of her career, had helped her to overcome her shyness and which now were part of her public persona.

But she wouldn't be wearing the glasses or a hat tonight. It was a long time since she had needed them to boost her confidence. She continued to wear them for a different reason. Without them she was seldom recognised as Andrina, the designer whose name was a byword for style. She could be herself, Maria Rawlings, and go about New York and London without being noticed and stared at as one of the leading trend-setters of the decade.

Six months ago, a profile writer in *Vogue* had written,

Andrina is a tastemaker, as influential as the legendary Eugenia Errazuriz who, in the thirties, gave a small swatch of fabric from her native Andes to the designer Schiaparelli who called it Shocking Pink and made a fortune from a new fashion colour. Andrina's origins are mysterious but are thought to be Central American. She refuses to talk about her background or her private life. It is doubtful if her punishing schedule allows any time for a private life. She is never seen at parties ...

But I shall be seen at a party tonight, thought Maria as, after signing her real name in the hotel register, she was taken up to her room.

That she was not on the exclusive guest list did not worry her. Security would be tight and all the other guests would have engraved invitations. But even without that essential piece of stiff white card requesting the pleasure of her presence, they could not turn her away. She had more right than anyone to be there.

If the security staff failed to recognise her, she would give them her professional card and insist they show it to Raul. He would be intrigued and have her brought to him. Then he would recognise her. Not, perhaps, at first glance. Not in the sophisticated, drop-dead dress contained in the black nylon hanging-bag now on its way up with the rest of her luggage in a separate service elevator.

But although it might take him a second or two to adjust to the way she looked now compared with her immature, ungroomed appearance seven years ago, there was no way he could have forgotten her.

Not because she had meant more to him than any of the other girls in his life. In that sense, as a passing fancy, she had been less memorable.

All the same Raul wouldn't have forgotten her. And she couldn't wait to see his face, not only when she first confronted him but later when, choosing her moment, she revealed him to the world in his true colours.

A few minutes before ten o'clock, Rosa, one of the chambermaids on duty on the fourth floor, returned to the narrow room where her friend Amparo was pressing a silk blouse for Room 402.

Both maids lived in a block of flats in one of the poorer *barrios* of the city and, when their shifts permitted, travelled to and from work on the same packed bus.

'What did 415 want?' Amparo asked, slipping the blouse on a hanger and inspecting it.

'Needed help with her dress. Chatted away, very friendly, while I was doing her up. Gave me a good tip too. She's only here for one night. Going to a do at the Prado.'

'José says there's a lot of important people in town for that.' Amparo's brother-in-law was a porter at the Ritz. 'Maybe she's someone famous.'

Before answering 415's bell, Rosa had checked the list of guests on their floor. 'Her name's Maria Rawlings. Señorita Rawlings. I've never heard that name. Have you?'

Amparo shook her head. 'What nationality is she? Rawlings sounds American or English.'

Although neither of them had ever left their native city, their work had extended their knowledge of the world, and given them insights into the lives and habits of the rich and privileged which had not always heightened their respect for the people they were paid to serve.

'Maybe her father was American and her mother was South American,' said Rosa. 'I couldn't quite place her accent, but Spanish was her first language. I'd bet on that. And I'll tell you something else. She was brought up properly. After I'd fastened her dress, I went into the bathroom to see if she needed fresh towels. You know what a mess some of them make...water everywhere...towels on the floor. Not this one. It was so neat and tidy you'd hardly have known she'd used it...except for the smell of her perfume. Lovely, it was. I'll have a dab of it later, when I'm turning down her bed.'

*   *   *

At that moment the subtle aroma of Maria's perfume was being enjoyed by the lift attendant who, while taking her down to the lobby, was discreetly weighing her up.

Like the maids, he was a shrewd judge of character and many of the hotel's guests would have been surprised at how much he could tell from the little he saw of them. Often his assessments were confirmed by the maids and waiters. The staff had an active grapevine.

Apart from stating which floor they wanted, a lot of the guests ignored him. But when the door had slid open to reveal this breathtaking blonde in evening dress, she had smiled and said, *'Buenas noches,'* before stepping in beside him.

Many beautiful girls stayed at the hotel, sometimes with husbands or parents and sometimes with men who were old enough to be their fathers or even grandfathers but who were not related to them. Girls of the latter type, if they used the lift without their escorts, would occasionally give him the eye.

But after her courteous greeting the gorgeous blonde remained silent, not admiring herself in the lift's mirrored walls as many pretty women did on their way down, but gazing at the door with the unfocused stare of someone with something on her mind. Although she wasn't twisting her rings or fidgeting with the cord of her silk purse, he sensed that she was in a state of controlled tension. Probably there would be a man waiting for her in the lobby. The liftman wished he were the one taking her out tonight. But he would never be able to afford her. The stones in her earrings weren't real, but even costume jewellery of that quality cost more than he earned in three months. As for the rest of her outfit, it would wipe out his wages for two years.

'Gracias.'

As the lift opened at the ground floor, she gave him another lovely smile. Not a mechanical smirk without really seeing him, but a proper smile with a look which made him feel he had registered with her; that she would know him again, not look through him as if he were invisible, the way guests often did if you happened to pass them in the street.

There was no one waiting for her in the lobby. But, as she crossed the polished marble floor to drop her room key through the slot on the porter's desk before turning towards the main entrance, his were not the only male eyes to follow her graceful figure on its way to the revolving doors. He noticed other men watching her leave the building.

As he turned back into the lift, he still had the feeling her air of self-possessed elegance was, in part, a façade. That girl had the jitters, he was sure of it. She was psyching herself up to meet someone or do something that frightened her. He couldn't imagine what it could be for she didn't look the sort to scare easily.

Maybe he'd see her again. He'd come on duty at eight and would go off at four. She ought to be back before then, unless whoever she was meeting persuaded her to spend the night at his place. But she didn't look the sort who would go to bed with a guy unless she was crazy about him, and those weren't the vibes he had been receiving while she was in the lift.

It could be she was on her way to commit a crime of passion, like the *madrileña* who had shot her two-timing lover in one of the city's best restaurants the year before. He hoped the blonde wasn't planning anything like that. It would be a shame for that lovely face and figure to be shut up in prison. She wouldn't look the same when she came out.

*   *   *

In the back of the taxi taking her to the Prado, Maria took several deep breaths to calm herself. Earlier today, she had been too busy, too rushed, to feel nervous. There had been a great deal to do after three weeks away. Even on the short flight from London she had been occupied with a backlog of paperwork.

But now there was nothing to distract her from the impending confrontation. Suddenly she was filled with misgivings. Was the impulsive decision to come here, made while she was still jet-lagged from the long flight from Indonesia, an act of madness? Would she regret it when her body and mind were back to normal?

Was it justice she wanted, or vengeance? Justice was a noble aim, revenge an ignoble one. In seeking to punish Raul, would she damage herself?

Now that it came to the point, her plan required more courage than she had realised. It would be so much easier to tap the driver on the shoulder and say she was feeling unwell and must return to the hotel.

But if she did that, if she ordered a meal from room service and spent the evening watching television, not only would it be a waste of several hundred pounds—money she could have spent on the homeless girls whose care was very important to her—but she would have to go on living with uncertainty. The uncertainty of not knowing whether Raul still had the power to excite her with a glance. Or whether, after seven years, and all she had learnt about men and life in the interim, she would look at him tonight and marvel at what her nineteen-year-old self had seen in him.

CHAPTER ONE

SOON after sunrise, when the only people on the beaches were darkly bronzed men raking the sand surrounding the thatched sunshades of the cabaña colonies, and a few white-skinned tourists whose body-clocks had not yet adjusted to the six-hour time-lag between Britain and the Caribbean seaboard of Mexico, Maria sailed along the coast to fetch the supplies and the mail.

She and her father, George Rawlings, had lived near Playa del Carmen since she was two years old. For most of her growing up years this stretch of the southern fringe of the Yucatán Peninsula had been untouched by tourism.

It was only since her sixteenth birthday, three years ago, that the greedy eyes of the resort developers had focused on these quiet beaches lapped by a turquoise sea teeming with coral formations and colourful fish.

For as long as Maria could remember the only access to the beach in front of their thatched hut had been by boat, or by a long bumpy dirt road leading to Highway 307, known as the Cancún-Tulum Corridor. It was called this because it connected Cancún, Mexico's newest and brashest resort, with Tulum, a fortified town built long ago by the Mayans and now a major tourist attraction.

Maria had never been to either place. Her father had turned his back on the world and kept her sequestered with him. It was only because he was not well that he had to allow her to come to town by herself.

'If anyone speaks to you, ignore them. Pretend you don't understand,' he had instructed her sternly.

12

What she did not understand was his hostility towards the *gringos*, the Mexican name for foreigners. Her father was himself a *gringo*: the son of an American father and British mother.

His wife, Maria's mother, had been Mexican, which was why Maria had dark brown eyes and black lashes. Her height and her hair were legacies from the great-grandparents who had gone to America from Norway in 1895.

Maria had a faded sepia photograph of the two determined young people who had set out to make their fortune in the New World, and whose descendents had inherited their long limbs and Nordic colouring.

Compared with the Mexicans and the Mayans, both people of small to medium stature, Maria often felt a giantess. Even barefoot she was inches taller than most local men. For much of her adolescence, had she had short hair instead of the sun-bleached mane which reached almost to her waist, she could have passed for a lanky boy.

To her relief, at fifteen she had begun to develop a more feminine shape. She would never have the full breasts and curvaceous hips and bottoms of the women of her mother's race or the tourists who, to her astonishment and her father's displeasure, lay on the sand almost naked.

'Sinvergüenzura . . . shamelessness!' he had muttered, the first time they had sailed past several semi-nude bathers disporting in the crystal shallows washing the pale coral sand of the first of the new cottage colonies.

Yet her father was not a prude. He had painted his wife without clothes and learnt his skills with pen and brush by drawing less beautiful bodies in the life classes at his art school. There were still a few drawings from that period of his life among the work in his portfolios.

Unfortunately Maria had not inherited his gift. Her only talent was for the bright embroidery which characterised the traditional Mexican dresses called *huipiles*.

But she wasn't wearing a *huipil* as she brought the dinghy inshore. From choice she would have worn shorts and a T-shirt today. But her father had insisted on her wearing a full skirt of drab brown cotton and a loose white cotton shirt. He had also made her plait her hair and fasten it in a prim loop secured with a piece of black tape.

A small boy she knew was searching the beach for discarded bottles. He responded to her whistle and came running to help her beach the dinghy.

'*Hola*! Maria. Is your *papá* still sick?'

'Yes.'

'He should see a doctor.'

'I know, but I can't persuade him. Keep an eye on the boat for me, Julio. I won't be more than an hour.'

'No problem.' Julio had picked up some English from the American tourists. The youngest of seven children, he had not been to school for six months because the place lacked a teacher. It made George Rawlings angry that millions of pesos were being spent on drains to serve the influx of tourists, but the children of Playa might remain uneducated for another six months.

Maria had completed her errands and was returning to the beach when a man lurched out of a bar and stepped in front of her.

'What's your hurry, babe? Where're y'goin'?' His speech was slurred, his eyes bloodshot. He was brandishing a bottle of Corona beer.

Maria had never had to contend with a drunk before. On rare occasions her father would spend an evening drinking tequila and next day would lie in his hammock instead of painting. But she had never seen him swaying from the knees like this man. She wasn't sure how to react. It seemed best to step to one side and hurry on her way.

To her dismay, as she dodged, the beer-drinker grabbed her by the arm, preventing her escape.

'You're cute. Why don' you and me get together an' have ourselves a party? I don't go for these Mexican chicks. Give me a blonde ev'ry time. You know why? Cos I'm a gennelman and, like the song says, gennelmen prefer blondes.'

Laughing uproariously, he began to weave down the street, his grasp sliding down to her wrist and forcing her to go with him.

Without much hope that he would respond, she tried a polite appeal.

'Please let me go, *señor*.'

'I'm not a *señor* and you're not a *señorita*. I'm from Detroit. Where're you from?'

Beginning to lose her temper, Maria was about to try the effect of swinging her bag of supplies against the bulge of slack flesh overhanging the belt of his trousers when another voice intervened.

'You're being a nuisance, *amigo*. Take your paw off the young lady's arm and beat it!'

Both the drunk and Maria looked around. Standing behind them, focusing a steely glare on the beer-drinker, was a tall, powerfully built man in a crisply laundered white *guayabera* and well-pressed white trousers.

For a moment the bloodshot eyes of the unshaven roughneck from Detroit held a belligerent gleam. Then he appeared to recognise that the other man was taller and fitter and, in spite of his immaculate clothes, looked a formidable adversary.

He decided to back down. 'OK...OK...take it easy, fella. Didn' mean no harm. Only tryin' to be frien'ly.'

As he reeled away Maria said gratefully, 'Thank you.'

'My pleasure,' said the tall man. 'Let me carry that bag. It looks too heavy for you.'

'Oh, no... please ... I can manage...'

But he had already taken hold of her laden bag of rice, maize and other staples and she wasn't sorry to surrender its weight. Already the sun was very hot. She was used to its burning rays, but now that the once quiet town was undergoing extensive building and drain-laying the air was full of dust and she was longing to cool off in the sea.

'You seem to have a lot of shopping? Are you here with a group? Staying at that place up the beach for back-packers?' he asked.

She knew where he meant. Often, on trips to town, she had looked wistfully at the young people who stayed there, spending the night in an open-sided dormitory where men and girls slept alongside each other in sky-blue and sea-green hammocks slung from treetrunk-thick poles under a thatched *palapa*. She envied their cama-raderie, their freedom to go where they pleased, to visit places like Tulum, and Cobá and Uxmal, the ancient cities of the Mayas which, after being lost for centuries, had been rediscovered and restored.

People came from all over the world to see them, es-pecially the fabulous city of Chichén Itzá. But Maria, although she lived less than a day's journey from them, had had to be content with reading about them.

In answer to the stranger's question, she said, 'No, I'm not a tourist. I live here... not here in Playa... but near.'

She wondered what brought him to Playa but was too shy to ask. It wasn't her nature to be shy, at least not with ordinary people, Mexican fishermen and shopkeepers and the countrywomen who came to Playa to sell produce.

But this man was different; like no one she had ever seen before. She wasn't even sure of his nationality. He had black hair and she could tell by the depth of his tan that his natural skin tone was the colour called olive.

But his eyes were a strange striking grey, and although he was dressed like an upper-class Mexican with expensive leather shoes and discreet bands of fine-drawn threadwork down the front of his *guayabera*, the cool yet formal shirt worn outside their trousers by professional men and everyone of importance, his accent was that of a foreigner.

As if he could read her mind, he said, 'I'm English, but my great-grandmother was Mexican and I like the climate of this country better than that of my own so I spend a lot of time here. How long have you lived in Mexico?'

'Always. My mother was Mexican.'

'Was?' he asked, and there was a kindness in his tone which made her warm towards him.

Even though she knew her father would disapprove of her talking to a man she didn't know, she said, 'She died when I was born, so I don't remember her.'

He frowned slightly. 'Are you an orphan?'

'Oh, no, I live with my father. He's American . . . like that man you got rid of . . . but much nicer,' she added, smiling.

'I should hope so. That guy was a lout. But all nations have their share of them,' he said, returning her smile.

It wasn't the first time in her life she had felt the sensations caused by being smiled at by an attractive member of the opposite sex. It had happened on several occasions when good-looking Mexican youths had flashed their white teeth and their dark eyes at her. But this time

the feeling of breathlessness and the stirring in the pit
of her stomach were stronger than ever before and she
felt herself starting to blush under his amused grey-eyed
scrutiny.

'I must run. I don't want to be late. My father will
worry if I'm not back when he expects me. Thank you
and goodbye, *señor*,' she said, reaching to retrieve her
bag.

But he would not release it. 'You can't run with this.
How did you get here? By boat?'

As they were walking in the direction of the beach he
had drawn the obvious conclusion.

'Yes, it's down there.' She pointed to where Julio was
keeping an eye on it for her. Then, as they came to the
top of a ramshackle flight of concrete steps overdue for
repair, she said, 'I can manage the rest of the way. You
can't walk on the sand in your good shoes.'

'Why not?' He went lightly down the steps, holding
the cumbersome bag as if it contained no more than a
few bananas and a loaf of the soft white bread, wrapped
in transparent plastic, that she had seen in a shop catering
to tourists.

Maria and her father ate tortillas like the Mexicans.
Strangely, although she *was* Mexican on her mother's
side, she never felt Mexican. Perhaps because she was
tall and had fair hair which didn't go with her brown
eyes and dark brows and lashes, she felt herself to be a
hybrid, different from her mother's people and equally
different from her father's. Nor, although she had always
lived here, did she feel a sense of belonging, that this
was her rightful place in the world. The truth, which she
never dared to express, was that she longed to get away,
to see all the places she had read about, not only the
cities of the past but the cities of the present: New
York...Paris...Madrid. Even to go to Cancún, less than

an hour's drive away, a place which had not existed in her mother's time, would be an adventure.

'My name is Raul. And yours?' the man asked.

'Maria...Maria Rawlings.'

Perhaps it was only her fancy, but she felt that her surname surprised him, although she had already said her father was American.

'Maria...it suits you,' he said. 'How old are you, Maria?'

'Nineteen.'

He raised an eyebrow. 'I would have thought not more than sixteen, if that. Where I come from, it takes a lot to make a girl of nineteen blush. They're women of the world at your age. But you look as innocent as your namesake.'

It took her a moment or two to grasp the allusion. When she did, she felt her cheeks burn for the second time.

'Perhaps you are,' he said, as they crossed the sand towards the dinghy. 'In which case your father should take better care of you. This town is beginning to attract some unsavoury types...worse than that slob you were having trouble with.'

'My father takes very good care of me. He's not well today. That's the only reason I'm here on my own. But anyway, I can look after myself,' she said, lifting her chin. 'If I'd hit that man with the bag, he'd have let go of me. He was so unsteady on his feet, he'd have fallen over.'

'Hmm...maybe. But it's better to avoid these contingencies. You were wandering along in a daydream. I was watching you before it happened. It pays to keep your wits about you, *chica*.'

Maria was often called *chica* by her father, who spoke Spanish as easily as English. But not with the upward inflection at the end of a sentence which was a characteristic of Mexican Spanish, at least among the ordinary people, although not perhaps among the rich and cultured of Mérida which had once been her mother's milieu.

But to be called 'girl' by one's parent was different from being addressed thus by mocking stranger. It made her feel like a child which was not how she wished to be seen. Conscious of her unbecoming clothes, the cheap rubber-soled *alpargatas* on her feet and of hair which had been smoothly brushed when she set out from home but had since been tangled by the breeze which had brought her here, suddenly she longed to be beautifully dressed and fastidiously groomed like the daughters of the rich.

Sometimes when they came to Playa, her father would buy a copy of *Diario de Quintana Roo* and read it while he drank a cold beer and Maria enjoyed the luxury of a glass of ice-cold orange juice.

Often the newspaper printed photographs of the first communion celebrations of children of socially prominent families, or of girls at a dance for the daughters of the élite. Girls of her age but as different from herself as she had been different from the children of the poorest people in Mexico, whose depths of poverty made her father grind his teeth with impotent rage.

'Do you come to Playa every day?' Raul asked her.

'No, only once or twice a month. We grow vegetables and the sea is full of fish.' Telling herself it was a courtesy, but knowing it was really curiosity, she asked, 'How long are you staying here?'

'My work has to do with the new resort being built a mile or so that way,' he said, with a nod in the opposite direction from the way she was going. 'I'll be around—on and off—until the work is completed. I don't suppose it will be finished on schedule but it's my job to see that it doesn't fall too far behind.'

'Are you the architect?'

'No, although I have studied architecture. You could say I was a trouble-shooter.'

She wasn't sure what he meant but was not going to reveal her ignorance by asking for an explanation, confirming his impression that she was a complete country bumpkin.

'Who's this?' Raul asked, as Julio climbed out of the beached dinghy in which he had been sitting, probably imagining that it belonged to him and he was sailing away on some high adventure.

Maria knew the boy shared her dreams of seeing the world. Perhaps, even though he was the youngest of seven children and went barefoot except on Sundays when he wore a pair of old plimsolls to accompany his parents to mass, Julio stood a better chance of fulfilling his ambitions than she did. He was what her father called street-wise, with a quick impudent wit and an eye to any opportunity to make a few pesos.

'This is my friend Julio Torres,' she said, in Spanish, because if Raul was working in Mexico he must be fluent in the language which had been his great-grandmother's native tongue. To the boy, she added, 'This is Don Raul...I don't know your last name, *señor*.'

'Raul Dysart.' He spelt it for them.

'I never heard that name before,' said Julio.

'It's an English name,' Raul told him. 'I have some Mexican blood but to all intents and purpose I'm a *gringo*,' he added, with another of his amused looks.

'You don't speak like a *gringo*...*señor*,' Julio tacked on politely.

He was a shrewd judge of a person's station in life and Maria could tell that, like the tipsy tourist, he recognised that Señor Dysart was someone it would be unwise to antagonise.

'I was born and grew up in England but I finished my education at the university in Mérida,' said Raul, dumping the bag of supplies in the dinghy, the dinghy being far enough out of the water for him to lean inboard without getting his feet wet. 'I had better give you a hand to get this tub afloat.' He stepped out of his polished loafers, showing spotless white socks which he peeled off and stuffed in one shoe.

To Maria's slight surprise his feet were as tanned as his face, neck and forearms, but his toenails were neatly clipped, not ragged and rimmed with dirt like many male toenails she saw. Her father's feet were always clean but even he had horny soles and coarse hairs on his toes and instep. She had never before seen a man's foot which pleased her eye and her gaze shifted to his hands, which were equally pleasing with long but wholly masculine fingers which looked strong enough to crush an apple to pulp yet capable of cradling a bird or a butterfly without damaging it.

She said, 'I am putting you to too much trouble, señor. Julio and I can manage. Please don't inconvenience yourself.'

'It's my privilege to be of assistance to you, señorita.'

In English his answer might have sounded exaggerated politeness, but not in Spanish. Both the words and the look which accompanied made her pulses race and her insides churn. But she knew he was only making fun of her. It would take someone far more beautiful and elegant than she could ever be to make him say that in all seriousness.

A few minutes later, when the dinghy was afloat and running free, Maria glanced back and saw that Raul was still watching her. As she looked at him, he raised his hand in a final wave before turning away and walking back up the beach with his shoes in his hand and Julio walking alongside, the difference in their heights making it necessary for the boy to tilt his head sideways to look up at him.

She wondered what they were talking about, the Mexican gutter-snipe and the Englishman whose bearing and manner sprang from generations of education and privilege.

Would she ever see Raul Dysart again? It seemed unlikely.

Now that he had explained what he was doing in these parts she ought not to want to see him again. He was one of the people who, in her father's opinion, were as ruthless and selfish as the owners of the great *haciendas* before the revolution. For generations they had ruled the land like feudal lords, keeping the people enslaved by a system which forced them to work for little reward and prevented them from seeking better conditions of employment.

Now, according to George Rawlings, a new breed of powerful men was exploiting the poor, using them to build and staff the rash of hugely profitable hotels and holiday complexes but not sharing the proceeds of tourism, not helping to provide education or better housing at the lowest level of society.

In her father's eyes, Raul Dysart would be as guilty of exploitation as the business barons and avaricious entrepreneurs.

Thinking about her father made her sigh. She loved him, and thought him a wonderful artist whose work would one day be valued as it deserved to be. But he wasn't an easy man to live with. He was moody and often irascible. She had to be careful not to upset him, never to argue with him. Time had not been kind to him. He looked older than his years and now bore little resemblance to photographs of himself as a young man. Looking at him now, it was hard to discern the charm which had caused her mother to fall madly in love, defying her parents' refusal to allow her to marry an unknown and penniless American artist who had come to Mexico because it was the birthplace of three of the twentieth century's greatest and most influential painters.

Unfortunately her father had never made a name for himself and, although he had an agent in New York who managed to sell a few of his paintings, the money they made was barely enough to cover their expenses.

Maria tried not to think about how she would survive if her father became seriously ill or died. She had never had any formal education because George Rawlings thought it unnecessary. He had taught her to read and write and to do mental arithmetic. Every day, from the age of ten, she had had to spend a hour studying a page in a single-volume encyclopaedia. It had taken her almost four years to progress from the town of Aachen to the last entry 'zygote', and then he had made her start again from the beginning.

But she did not share his confidence that all the information she had committed to memory would help her to earn her living if that became necessary.

About a week later, she was lying in her hammock, swinging gently from side to side and watching a cruise ship passing on the horizon, when the angry buzz of a speedboat caught her attention.

It was inside the reef, skimming over the water where she spent hours of her life floating face down, watching the shoals of gauzy-finned fish. The only person in the boat was the man at the wheel and at first, because of his black hair and the burnished bronze of his skin, she took him for a local. But then as the boat slowed down, its white wake narrowing, something about him seemed familiar. As the motor cut out and the boat swung inshore, she drew in a breath of surprise and recognition.

It was Raul Dysart...coming here!

Had Julio told him where she lived? What did he want? How would her father react to a visit from a stranger? Would he be angry that she hadn't mentioned the circumstances in which she had met Raul?

Putting her feet to the floor on either side of the *hamaca*, Maria stood up and swung one long slender leg over the top of the swag of faded blue threads which was her bed and her chair.

The Rawlingses had few possessions. Her father had his easel and his painting equipment, and Maria had a trunk full of books he had mail-ordered for her. In all other respects they lived like the poorest Mexicans, except that, being close to the sea, they were able to keep themselves cleaner than people living inland where water was scarce. Even here, water to drink and cook with was a precious commodity, never to be wasted.

'Who the hell is this?' said her father, emerging from the hut, its walls made of wooden stakes with a coating of adobe applied on the inside.

He had been having a nap but must have been roused by the noise of the powerboat's engine and was glowering irritably at the man who by now had secured the boat with an anchor and was about to wade ashore.

Today Raul was wearing shorts and carrying something which, as he put it on, proved to be a white tee-shirt.

Maria said hurriedly, 'He's English. I—I forget to tell you. There was a drunk in Playa the other day. He was making a nuisance of himself and this man—Mr Dysart—told him off.'

George Rawlings gave her a sharp look. 'Did he ask where you lived? Did you tell him?'

'No...but perhaps Julio told him. I'd left him minding the boat and Mr Dysart insisted on carrying my shopping. He has very nice manners.'

'Some of the world's worst scoundrels have perfect manners,' her father said sourly. 'Is he on vacation?'

Knowing that if she told him the truth, he would send Raul away, perhaps even be abusive, Maria said, 'I don't know. We didn't have much conversation.'

The lie brought a guilty flush to the skin below her high cheekbones. But fortunately her father's gaze was fixed on the man approaching them and he didn't notice her unease.

'Holds himself well...not a sloucher,' he said, as Raul came nearer. A tall, upright man himself—although not as tall as their visitor—one of the bees in his bonnet was the posture of many of his daughter's generation who, according to him, never stood up straight if there was a wall to lean against or somewhere to lounge with their feet up.

'Good morning, Mr Rawlings. My name is Dysart,' said Raul, coming to a halt just outside the shade cast by their thatched *palapa*. 'I'm told you're an artist, sir. I hope you don't mind my intrusion on your privacy, but I'm looking for paintings to buy and heard you might have some to sell.'

He took no notice of Maria. She might have been invisible.

'Who told you that?' asked her father.

'A man at a shop in Playa when I asked if he knew of any artists in this area.'

'You're a dealer?'

'No, a collector...an admirer of Orozco, Rivera and Siqueros.'

To her father, the three great Mexican muralists were like gods. Raul could not have said anything better calculated to ingratiate himself, but there was no way he could have known that.

However there was no noticeable warming of Rawlings's expression as he said gruffly, 'It's easy to admire artists when the whole world has acknowledged their stature... not so easy to recognise talent before its time. I don't sell my work here. It goes to a gallery in New York.'

'I see. In that case I've disturbed you unnecessarily. My apologies. I wouldn't have come here uninvited except that one day last week I was able to be of some slight assistance to your daughter.' He glanced at her. 'Hello again.' He made her feel ten years old, a child whose presence must be briefly acknowledged but not of the smallest interest to him.

Returning his attention to her father, he said, 'I go to New York from time to time. At which gallery is your work shown, Mr Rawlings?'

Her father said, 'I'll write it down for you. Fetch some paper and a pencil, Maria.'

As she obeyed, she heard Raul say, 'I was told that you lived very simply, without a generator. I took the liberty of bringing a cooler box of cold beer and some cans of soft drinks for your daughter. May I bring it ashore?'

She held her breath for a moment, fearing that her father, with his low opinion of the human race in general, might not take this gesture at its face value but suspect some ulterior motive and respond with an abrasive refusal.

To her relief, his answer was, 'That was thoughtful of you. Having missed my trip to town last week, I could do with a cold beer.'

Raul had gone to fetch the cooler when she brought her father a piece of scrap paper and a pencil. He said, 'Can we offer him something to eat?'

Being early risers, they had their main meal at noon and a lighter snack about sundown. Sometimes, for an hour after dark, they read by the light of a butane gas lamp, keeping the mosquitoes at bay by burning a coil of clay impregnated with a repellent, and later letting down nets to shroud their hammocks. In the night she was often disturbed by her father's snoring or by the incoherent mumbles he made in his sleep. Often he couldn't sleep and through the veil of the netting she would see him pacing the beach by the water's edge, a gaunt figure casting a long black shadow on the sand.

'Yes, there's enough food for three.'

She went away to prepare it, looking forward to the luxury of a cold drink with her food.

Whether Raul would find the simple fare they lived on palatable was another matter. If he didn't, he wouldn't show it. But she couldn't rely on her father being equally punctilious and dreaded the moment when he found out what Raul was doing in Mexico. Was there some way she could warn him to skirt the subject? She couldn't think of one. It was sure to come up sooner or later and, when it did, George Rawlings's unusual amiability would instantly dissipate. The fact that Raul was a guest wouldn't restrain him from venting his hatred of everyone involved in the coast's development. He would probably lose his temper and instinct told her Raul was not a man to accept the sort of tongue-lashing her father was capable of inflicting.

When she returned from the primitive kitchen under a smaller *palapa* at the back of their main living quarters, her father was sitting sideways in his hammock, taking sips from the neck of a bottle of Corona beer, and Raul was occupying her hammock.

He rose as she joined them and would have lowered his long frame to the ground had her father not said, 'Don't disturb yourself. We have more than two *hamacas*. She can sling another for herself.'

He indicated the stout ring bolts driven at Maria's head height into all the thick uprights supporting the roof. They allowed hammocks to be slung in various positions, in shade or sunlight. During the day they usually sat with the feet of their hammocks tied to the same post and the head-hooks in rings about ten feet apart. This was how the hammocks were slung now.

Taking down a third *hamaca* hanging in a loop from another upright, she slung it on the far side of her father's hammock and a little distance apart from the two men so that she could listen and observe from the background.

Whenever her father talked about her mother, Isela, he emphasised her how shy and modest she had been when he met her, how different from modern Mexican girls with their high heels, short skirts and painted faces. He had raised Maria to feel that a woman's rightful place was in the background, attending to domestic matters while men discussed serious issues and took all the important decisions. As a child she had accepted this view, but for several years now rebellious feelings had been stirring inside her. Now, sitting quietly by, waiting for her father to invite Raul to eat with them, she found herself resenting the way they both ignored her presence. True, Raul had stood up for her, but that had been an automatic reflex which didn't extend to including her in the conversation or addressing his remarks to her as well as her father.

'When I came here twenty years ago, this was a paradise,' George Rawlings was saying. 'Even after Jacques Cousteau filmed the Palancar Reef over by Cozumel——' he waved his hand towards the offshore island marked by a few tall buildings on the horizon '—it was a long time before tourism reared its ugly head. Now it's just a matter of time before this whole coast is desecrated.'

Raul nodded. 'But the Mexican government does seem aware of the ecological dangers and the need to control development.'

George Rawlings gave an impatient growl. 'That doesn't mean they'll resist the commercial pressures.'

Before her father could mount his hobby-horse, Maria surprised herself by saying, 'May we offer you lunch, Mr Dysart? We're only having *motuleños* and fruit, but there's more than enough for three if you'd care to share it?'

For an instant, she thought that, put out by her un-wonted boldness, her father might rescind the invitation. He was capable of it. But he said nothing, nodding his head as Raul gave his host an enquiring glance before replying, 'That's very kind of you. I'd be delighted.'

During the simple meal served on a trestle table where the two men shared the bench and Maria perched on a stool, the men talked about modern art.

Although Raul ate his fried eggs bedded on tortilla and bean paste, garnished with cheese and peas and topped with tomato sauce, with apparent enjoyment, she wished he had come yesterday when they had eaten fresh fish.

Presently, as they were finishing the meal with a salad of papaya, pineapple and water-melon, he said, 'It wasn't only my interest in your paintings which brought me here, Mr Rawlings. In a couple of weeks' time, an elderly relation of mine is coming from England to tour the ruins of the Mayan cities. She's my father's aunt, a maiden lady in her late seventies whose spirit of adventure has been known to outstrip her strength. As I've seen the ruins many times and have commitments which prevent me from doing the tour with her, I'm looking for someone else to go with her.'

For the first time since his arrival, he looked intently at Maria.

Then, turning back to her father, he went on, 'It occurred to me, after our meeting in Playa last week, that, if you could spare her for two weeks, your daughter would be an ideal companion and interpreter. Many young women would find my aunt rather trying, and she wouldn't enjoy their company. She's rather strait-laced and pernickety, but I'm attached to her and want to make her visit as pleasant and memorable as possible.'

Maria held her breath. She didn't mind how difficult the old lady was. It was a chance to see the fabulous lost cities now partially restored to their former magnificence. But would her father let her take this wonderful opportunity?

Holding her breath, she waited for his reaction. She knew it would be useless to show her eagerness and beg him to agree. Her wishes wouldn't influence him. It all depended on whether, as seemed to be the case, he had taken a liking to Raul.

'Naturally you would want to satisfy yourself that your daughter would be in good hands,' said Raul. 'I can provide unimpeachable references which there will be time for you to check. My aunt always travels as comfortably as possible and would give Maria ample pocket money. She's old-fashioned but not ungenerous.'

Oh, please, Father...*please* say yes, was Maria's silent prayer.

George Rawlings looked at her and then at his tall, black-haired guest. His expression was dubious. 'I need Maria here. I'm working on an important picture. I haven't time to mess about cooking and cleaning.'

Her heart sank. Once her father had made up his mind, nothing would budge him.

'Isn't there a local woman who would look after you?' Raul suggested. 'We'd be pleased to pay any out-of-pocket expenses. I believe your daughter is uniquely qualified to supply my great-aunt's needs. Her companion has to be completely bilingual, intelligent, *persona de cultura* and, above all, patient with an amiable but somewhat eccentric old lady. It won't be easy to find another girl with those qualities.'

Rawlings snorted. 'Impossible! But that's no reason why I should put myself out.'

Something came over Maria. She sat up very straight, her expression suddenly resolute. 'I want to go, Father. I've always wanted to see Chichén Itzá and the other cities. You left me with Rosalba when you had to go to America last year. She'll look after you while I'm gone. It's only for two weeks. I'm sure Mamá would have said I should go.'

Her father looked astonished. Even Raul seemed slightly surprised, as if he had decided she was a submissive creature who would never stand up for herself. She felt a rush of satisfaction at having at last asserted herself. But what if her father put his foot down? Did she have the courage to disobey if he forbade her to go? Would Raul's aunt take her without her father's approval?

'I'll think about it,' he said. 'It's time for my siesta. Come back in a day or two, Dysart. I'll let you know my decision then.'

CHAPTER TWO

'CHANGED his mind, by the look of it,' said George Rawlings, some days later. 'Or found someone else. There'd be plenty of volunteers if he spread the word.'

'Perhaps the final decision will be made by his great-aunt,' said Maria. 'If I were an elderly lady, I shouldn't want someone I had never met foisted on me.'

When, yesterday, there had been no sign of the speedboat returning, and this morning had gone by without the drone of an engine to make her heart beat in excited anticipation, she had begun to lose hope of seeing him again.

As her father said, there must be dozens of girls in Playa del Carmen and elsewhere who would jump at the chance to look after old Miss Dysart while she visited the lost cities of the Mayas.

Not surprisingly, after Raul's departure, her father had been annoyed with Maria for speaking out. But not as angry as she had feared he might be. And when she had stuck to her guns despite his annoyance, he had gradually come round to the view that it might not be a bad thing for her to broaden her experience of the world in the protective company of an elderly English spinster.

But now it appeared that Raul had changed his mind. Maria wanted the job so badly that she was tempted to go to Playa and seek him out. Probably he was staying at the Continental Plaza, a huge hotel by the ferry dock which made her father fulminate every time he saw it. She could imagine how he would react when he found out that Raul was involved in the building of an even larger resort complex.

There had been a brief refreshing shower of rain and the sky held the promise of a beautiful sunset when her ear caught a sound which made her put down the shirt she was mending and look eagerly in the direction of Playa.

She was alone. Her father had gone for the long walk he took every afternoon after four o'clock when the sun had lost its fierce heat.

At first the craft making the noise which had alerted her was too far away for her to be sure it *was* Raul coming back. It was two or three minutes before she could be certain.

Then, with only a few minutes to spare before he was close enough to see her, she leapt out of her hammock and rushed to put on a clean shirt and the blue denim skirt her father had brought back from his trip to America.

There was just time to comb her hair and pull it through an elasticated ruffle of printed cotton, bought on the same trip, before she heard the motor cut out and knew that Raul was almost here.

She would have liked to run down to the water's edge to greet him and tell him that, if the offer was still open, her father had agreed to let her go.

But, having mentally rehearsed this third encounter many times since his previous visit, she had decided that, in case he had changed his mind, it would be less embarrassing for them both if she didn't seem too eager.

'Good afternoon, Mr Dysart,' she said formally, as he came up the beach, carrying the large blue plastic cool-box he had brought before.

He smiled at her, his teeth as white against his tan as those of the Mexican youths who sometimes, early in the morning, came by with their throw-nets. In the short time since his last visit—although it had seemed an interminable interval to her—his tan seemed to have deepened.

'Hi! How's it going?'

His casual greeting made her feel as if she were entering her teens rather than leaving them.

'We're both well, thank you. My father's not here at the moment, but he won't be long. Would you like some tea? We have camomile or *jamaica*.' In case he had never tried it, she added, 'It's made from hibiscus flowers.'

'Thanks, but I brought some cold drinks: beer for your father, Sprite and orange juice for you. Has he made up his mind?'

She nodded, trying to sound calm and composed as she said, 'If you still feel I'm the most suitable candidate, he has come round to the view that it would be a good experience for me.'

'In that case it's settled,' he said. 'Provided your father is satisfied with our references. Naturally he'll want to be sure that you're being entrusted to people who will take good care of you. Where did you go to school?'

Maria felt a thrust of panic. If she told him she had never been to school would he change his mind? Was this chance, now within her grasp, about to be snatched away?

It was impossible to pretend she had been properly educated because she didn't know the names of any schools. Besides fabrications didn't come easily to her. Or deliberate omissions. Not telling her father that she had met Raul had weighed on her conscience. She didn't want to start off on the wrong foot with Raul.

'I haven't been to school,' she admitted. 'My father thought a private education was preferable to sending me away. I haven't any paper qualifications but I'm quite widely read and I've taught myself to read French. I'm not sure how well I can speak it. My father doesn't and I've never met any French tourists.'

'Living here, I shouldn't think you meet many tourists of any nationality, do you?'

'Not often. Occasionally a back-packer or two comes by...or someone on horseback. We don't encourage them to call. Father dislikes being disturbed when he's working. Here he comes now.'

Raul glanced along the beach to where her father was bending to examine something washed up by the sea. As they watched, he resumed his walk. Not for the first time Maria noticed that his once limber stride had, on the return walk, deteriorated into a trudge. Seen from a distance he looked older than his years. She felt a pang of anxiety. What if, while she was away, he was taken ill and needed her? Rosalba would take care of his meals and the cleaning, but then she would go back to her own place in a clearing a mile up the track. He would be alone here all night.

But she didn't yet know that she was going. Raul had said it was settled, but that was before she had revealed her lack of education.

'Aunt Iris speaks French,' he told her. 'You and she have a good deal in common. She was the only girl in her family. While her five brothers were at school, she stayed at home being taught by a French governess. She also had a lonely childhood and grew up to be a shy girl. Do you know what a débutante was?'

Maria nodded. 'An upper-class girl who made her début in society by being presented at court in England, or at a cotillion ball in America, and then spent a year going to parties and dances, hoping someone eligible would propose to her.'

'That's right. My great-aunt was a very shy girl, and not pretty. Her début was an unhappy time for her. She didn't receive any proposals, then or later. She was born at a time when a woman had to be exceptionally strong-minded to assert her independence. You can probably empathise with her better than most girls of your age because your father appears to have dominated your life in the way fathers did when she was young. I think you'll get on very well. It was a stroke of luck that I met you in Playa last week. Otherwise I should have felt obliged to escort her myself and I can't really spare the time at present.'

Maria found this statement oddly deflating. Clearly his only interest was in her usefulness in a particular situation. What other interest did she expect or want? He was much older than she was, at least thirty, and his world was as different from hers as the glittering night-life on board the great cruise liners was unlike her own short lamplit evenings, reading or playing chess with her father. If all went well, she would have a brief glimpse of the life women led in Raul's world. But it wouldn't last long and afterwards she would probably never see him again.

'When do you expect your great-aunt to arrive?' she asked.

'After I've spoken to your father, I'll put the arrangements in hand immediately. It's only a matter of booking her flight to Cancún. It's not a place she'll like but there are comfortable hotels where she can spend a couple of days resting. Elderly people usually take longer than young ones to recover from jet lag and she'll have to adjust to the time difference.'

He glanced at the watch strapped to his wrist, the strong wrist of a man accustomed to physical exertion as well as desk work. 'In England they're six hours ahead of us,' he said. 'There, it's eleven o'clock. She'll be asleep.'

'Why won't your aunt like Cancún?' Maria asked.

Her father regarded the town as an abomination, but he had no time for any cities, even romantic-sounding places like Paris and Venice and Istanbul. 'Sinks of human degradation!' was how he described them. She could not believe they were as horrible as he made out.

'Cancún is for people who want to spend a holiday swimming and sunbathing, shop for souvenirs in air-conditioned malls, spend Happy Hour drinking margaritas, and dance in discos at night,' Raul explained. 'There's nothing wrong with that. The people who look down their noses at that sort of holiday usually have more money and time, and less stressful lives, than the people who flock to Cancún to enjoy themselves. Aunt Iris prefers quieter places with some historical or archi-tectural interest.'

By now her father was only a hundred yards away and the Englishman gave him a friendly wave. George Rawlings responded, but not in the manner of a man seeing a welcome visitor.

Maria had an ominous feeling that he might have been thinking things over and changed his mind.

'Would you like to see Cancún?' Raul asked her. 'I could arrange for you to meet my aunt there, or you can be picked up from Playa del Carmen. The first ancient city she wants to see is Tulum, further down Highway 307.'

Maria would have liked to see Cancún for herself, but she thought it prudent to say, 'I don't think my father wants me to be away for any longer than is necessary. If I could be picked up from Playa it would be better.'

'As you wish.' He moved away to meet the older man. 'Good afternoon, Mr Rawlings.'

*   *   *

Two weeks later the Rawlingses arrived at Playa del Carmen to go to the Hotel Molcas where Raul would introduce them to Miss Iris Dysart and her tour guide who would also be driving the car her great-nephew had organised for her.

By now Maria felt fairly sure that her father wasn't going to change his mind about letting her go. She knew she wouldn't feel completely sure until they had said goodbye and she was on her way, and her excitement was marred by the feeling that perhaps she ought not to be deserting him.

Her clothes and other belongings were packed in the roll-bag George Rawlings had bought for his trip to America. He had given her the money to buy herself a new blouse and skirt and a pair of flat-heeled shoes, not as good as those she had seen on the better-dressed tourists, but more respectable-looking than *hauraches*.

'I've never seen you looking so smart, Maria,' said Julio, who had seen their boat and run down to the water's edge to earn a few pesos minding it for them. '*Muy guapa!*' he added, with a grin.

She laughed and pretended to aim a cuff at him. 'Save your compliments for the tourists.'

'Where are you going all dressed up?'

'To look after a lady who's come to see the cities of long ago. I'll be away for ten days.'

'If you please her, perhaps she'll give you a permanent job. It's not bad being a maid.'

Catching this last remark, her father said sharply to her in English, 'Why did you tell the boy you were going to be a maid? You'll be a companion...an amanuensis...not a maid. Always remember that your mother came from one of the best families in Mérida.'

His annoyance seemed inconsistent considering he claimed to believe that people who did menial work were as worthy of respect as those they served.

But she said obediently, 'Yes, Father.' It wouldn't do to annoy him at this eleventh hour.

The Hotel Molcas was a modest establishment compared with the ostentatious opulence of the recently-built Continental Plaza on the other side of the ferry dock. Tables were set for lunch on the smaller hotel's veranda and in the interior dining-room and Raul was waiting for them at the entrance.

Briefly scrutinising Maria's neat appearance, he greeted them both before saying, 'The car is round the corner. Shall we put the bag with my aunt's luggage? She's washing her hands.'

On the way to the car, he added, 'There's been a slight hitch in our arrangements. Unfortunately the guide is unable to join us until tomorrow. As it was difficult if not impossible to make contact with you from Cancún and tell you we should be starting out a day late, I shall be doing the driving as far as Cobá and the guide will meet us there tomorrow morning.'

Although this alteration of the plan might be inconvenient to him, to Maria it was good news. It meant she would be starting the trip with someone she knew, if only slightly, rather than two complete strangers. There was another reason why it pleased her, but she chose to ignore that.

The vehicle in which they were to travel was not one of the Chevrolet ranch waggons from which she had sometimes seen small groups of tourists disgorging. Nor was it one of the long showy cars Julio said were called limos which, outmoded, battered and rusty, ended their lives parked outside overcrowded houses at the back of the fishing port, the part most tourists never saw.

This was a comfortable but not ostentatious car with a capacious trunk already containing a large suitcase and a matching smaller soft-topped case, both with 'Miss Iris Dysart' but no address written on the leather-edged labels.

Her father placed her flight bag beside them and Raul relocked the trunk.

'Are you excited, Maria?' he asked, looking down at her.

'Yes.'

It was the kind of question one asked a child, not a grown-up person, she thought vexedly, as they returned to the hotel. But this evening she meant to surprise him. If the books she had read were a reliable guide to the manners and mores of people like his great-aunt, Miss Dysart would change for dinner and Maria meant to put up her hair and wear her best *huipil*. Then perhaps he would realise that she wasn't as childlike as he seemed to think.

Miss Dysart was sitting at one of the veranda tables, watching people buying tickets from the kiosks of two rival ferry companies. She was not as old-ladyish as Maria had expected. Obviously she *was* old, but not in a stout, slow-moving, short-sighted way.

Instead she was tall and spare, her face a mesh of fine lines and her hair an astonishing, outrageous shade of red. Maria had seen elderly tourists with what her father called bottle-blonde hair and even some wearing wigs. She had never before seen a woman in her seventies with bottle-red hair. Fortunately Raul introduced her father first. By the time it was her turn to shake hands, she had masked her astonishment.

'How d'you do?' said Miss Dysart, looking her up and down with an inscrutable expression which did not reveal her immediate reaction to Maria's appearance.

'Shall we have lunch out here, or would you rather eat inside, Mr Rawlings?'

'Whichever you prefer,' said her father.

Although his manner was courteous, Maria had the feeling he hadn't taken to Miss Dysart, perhaps because of her flamboyant hair.

'It's not the peaceful place it once was...before the developers got their hands on it,' he added, scowling at the sight of a labourer going past with a pick on his shoulder.

'Most places aren't,' said Miss Dysart. 'My own village in England has changed out of all recognition. I preferred it as it was. But my elders said the same thing when I was a young woman and so, no doubt, did the ancient Mayans in their time. Eventually, of course, their civilisation collapsed. Perhaps ours is going the same way. But I don't feel inclined to dwell on that at the moment...having escaped from a cold, wet, depressing English winter into this glorious weather. But I know it's not always thus. Were you here when Hurricane Gilbert swept across this peninsula?'

While George Rawlings was describing the devastation wreaked by the hurricane, a waiter came to give them each a menu and enquire if they wished for drinks.

Raul looked questioningly at his aunt who said, 'Water, please?' and then at Maria who said,

'And for me, please.'

'But not carbonated,' added Miss Dysart, before turning back to the older man. 'What would you recommend me to eat, Mr Rawlings?'

'I can't advise you. I never eat here. My daughter's an excellent cook and we don't patronise restaurants,' he answered.

'In that case Raul will advise me. Being unmarried, he frequently eats in restaurants...as I do myself,' said

Miss Dysart. 'Until a few years ago I had someone to cook for me. It's a skill I never acquired.'

'Try the *pollo píbil*,' said Raul. 'It's chicken cooked in a banana leaf with an orange sauce. What would you like, Maria?'

'May I have *panuchos*, please?'

'I'll have the same. And you, Mr Rawlings?'

'*Poc chuc*,' her father said tersely, his manner making her feel that something about the Dysarts made him resentful and angry; that even now, with her baggage already in the car and her accommodation booked, he was capable of changing his mind.

Then what would happen? Would Miss Dysart insist the commitment be honoured? Perhaps, although she concealed it, she wasn't taken with them and would just as soon not have Maria as her companion. Even though she didn't speak Spanish, she looked capable of making herself understood without it.

Before they met, Maria had visualised herself looking after a nervous elderly person who would mislay her spectacles, need help going up and down steps and expect her cases to be packed and unpacked for her.

Miss Dysart's spectacles were attached to a cord round her neck and she looked neither frail not unsteady on her feet. What services would she need that couldn't be performed by the staff at the hotels?

If her father did change his mind, Miss Dysart would probably say, 'By all means keep your daughter at home with you, Mr Rawlings. She looks more of a liability than an asset. I can manage very well without her.'

In any other circumstances Maria would have enjoyed eating a meal she had not had to cook, at an elegantly laid table, with the comings and goings of holiday-makers and local people providing a passing show of the kind she loved to watch.

As it was she was too much on edge to enjoy it to the full. She was also unhappily aware of making little or no contribution to the conversation. With Rosalba and Julio she could gossip and joke, but at the moment tension was making her tongue-tied.

To her surprise, Miss Dysart suddenly said, 'I'm glad to find you aren't a chatterbox, Maria. Raul assured me you weren't, but the younger generations of my family only stop talking when they're listening to pop on their head-sets. I travel with a head-set myself but I prefer classical music. What is that I can hear playing now?'

'It's a *marimba*—a type of xylophone—being played in the plaza round the corner to put the tourists from the cruise ships in a spending mood,' Raul said drily.

'Rather catchy,' said Miss Dysart, tapping out the beat on the tablecloth.

She was not the only one to respond to the infectious rhythm. Maria's feet had been tapping under the table and a girl who was passing the restaurant was clicking her fingers and swaying her hips to the beat.

She was with a group of young travellers, probably from one of the hammock dormitories. As she sashayed past, she glanced at the four people lunching and flashed a smile at Raul.

Maria didn't know whether he too had been watching the girl. But he caught the smile and reacted to it by smiling back and raising his beer glass slightly, a clear signal of admiration for her looks and her uninhibited *joie de vivre*.

Maria looked at the girl again, envying her self-confidence and her freedom to express her personality in that bizarre yet pleasing outfit. She had on a red cotton bodice, the kind worn by Indian women under their saris, with a piece of patterned material tied sarong-fashion round her hips leaving her brown midriff bare. A straw hat adorned with a bright scarf, dangling earrings and a wristful of bracelets completed her outfit. Clearly she was a free spirit who, seeing a good-looking man in the company of two older people, and a dowdy girl with dull clothes and no make-up, saw no reason not to smile at him.

Maria wondered if, had Raul been on his own, he would have invited the girl to join him for a beer. Probably not. She might be travelling alone, or one of the men in the group might be her boyfriend. Anyway, although she was attractive, she didn't seem the type to catch his eye more than momentarily. His women would be more sophisticated. Or perhaps, wherever he was based, he had a beautiful permanent girlfriend, someone with an interesting career and a background similar to his own.

When the time came to say goodbye, her father shook hands with the others before saying gruffly to her, 'Goodbye, girl. Have a good time.'

He had never been a demonstrative man or used endearments or pet names, not even when she was little. But she felt sure he loved her even if he couldn't show it. Perhaps the pain of losing her mother had made him afraid of exposing his deepest feelings.

She said, 'Take care of yourself, Papá.' And then, on impulse, she added, 'I love you very much,' and flung her arms round him.

He didn't return her hug, but his voice sounded husky as he said, 'Off you go. Don't keep them waiting.'

For Miss Dysart was now in the car with Raul holding the door open for Maria to join his great-aunt in the back.

It was typical of George Rawlings that he didn't wait to see the car move off, but was already walking back

towards the beach when Maria turned to give him a final
wave. She wondered if he also had tears in his eyes and
blinked hers back before turning to face the front seat.
Catching sight of Raul's grey eyes reflected in the rear-
view mirror and watching her, she hoped he couldn't see
she was upset. She didn't want to be thought a cry-baby.

'I expect your father will miss you, but he has his
painting to occupy him and you have your own life to
lead,' said Miss Dysart. 'I often wish I'd been born a
few generations later. At your age I longed for adventures but had to wait until I was middle-aged before I
could go where I pleased. What is your plan for the
future, Maria?'

'I haven't one. My father needs me to keep house for
him. Some day he'll be recognised as a very fine painter.

'You may be right. But you must find your own métier,
not spend your life serving his,' said Miss Dysart firmly.
'Raul, stop the car, would you? As you tell me the
scenery from here to Tulum is much the same as it was
on the road from Cancún, in other words rather boring,
Maria can come in the front with you while I put my
feet up and study my guide-book.'

Raul brought the car to a standstill and got out to
open the rear offside door and then the front nearside
door. Whether he minded having Maria foisted on him
was impossible to say. Clearly, if Miss Dysart had been
down-trodden in her youth, she was making up for it
now by saying what she thought and doing as she pleased
without much regard for anyone else's wishes.

Maria wondered if Raul was genuinely fond of her,
or if his great-aunt was rich and he had expectations of
a large legacy when she died. She had read about ulterior motives in books but had never met anyone who
had them in real life. But then how many people had

she met? She knew her experience of human behaviour was extremely limited.

As the farthest she had ever travelled was by the ferry to Cozumel, where her father had painted some seascapes on the undeveloped east coast of the once-sacred island, she didn't find Highway 307 as boring as Miss Dysart had.

True, it ran almost dead straight, bordered on either side by thick scrubby vegetation which here and there was being bulldozed in preparation for development. But for her this was unknown territory and, now she was on her way, she was determined to enjoy every minute.

After a period of silence, Raul gave her a sideways glance and said, 'The hotels where you'll be staying all have pools for guests to cool off after the day's sightseeing. Did you bring a swimsuit with you? Perhaps, living where you do, you don't bother to wear one.'

'Yes, I do...and I've brought it,' she answered. 'There's a nude beach between us and Playa but the village people don't like it. They think it's embarrassing to lie about with nothing on. A girl who came by once— a traveller—told me it's common in Europe. Everyone does it there, she said.'

'They don't strip off altogether as on the nude beach near you. That's still confined to special beaches. But topless sunbathing doesn't raise any eyebrows. Now it's the fashion to show off the female backside...which is fine if it's a nice shape, but not so good if its owner has a cellulite problem.'

'What's cellulite?'

She saw his mouth twitch with amusement.

'I was forgetting that you don't speak the jargon of the fashion magazines. Cellulite is a fancy name for fat, especially flab on hips and thighs. Not something you have to worry about,' he added, taking his eyes off the road to scan the lines of her figure.

It wasn't the way he had looked at the girl in the hat. His admiring appraisal of her shape had been like a visual caress. Maria felt he looked at her as if she were a stray cat or an undernourished child.

They arrived at the hotel at Cobá, where they were spending the first night, late in the afternoon. A porter whose features, particularly the curved bridge of his nose, indicated that he was a descendant of the Mayans whose city lay hidden in the jungle near by, hurried out of the building to attend to their luggage.

'Would you like to have tea first, Aunt Iris? Or would you prefer to go to your room?' asked Raul, as he steered them into the restful dimness of a hallway surrounding a small patio planted with creepers and ferns with a fountain splashing into a series of basins.

'Tea would be most acceptable,' said his aunt. 'But I thought this hotel was under French management. Will they serve tea?'

'It's run by Club Med but they cater to all nationalities. Find somewhere comfortable to sit while I sign the register.' He went off to attend to the formalities.

'Let's explore,' said Miss Dysart, following the highly polished dark red tiles paving the entrance hall and continuing round either side of the patio.

Very soon they discovered another much larger patio surrounded on three sides by guest rooms and on the fourth by sunny and shady sitting areas. In the centre was the swimming-pool, surrounded by tropical plants. At the moment there was no one in it and Maria longed to dive into its invitingly clear, calm depths but knew that must wait until she had performed whatever duties Miss Dysart required of her.

'We'll sit there,' said the Englishwoman, leading the way to a *palapa* overlooking the pool where brightly cushioned banquettes and rustic tub chairs invited relaxation. 'Ah, here comes Raul ... and our tea. Everyone jumps to his bidding. Whenever I've travelled with him, it has all gone like clockwork ... most relaxing.'

'Tired?' he asked, as he joined them.

'A little, yes,' she agreed. 'Tulum was fascinating. I shouldn't have minded living there. A small walled city overlooking the sea ... delightful. Didn't you think so, Maria?'

'Yes, it was a lovely place.'

'And you look as fresh as a daisy,' said Miss Dysart, smiling at her. 'But I'm not accustomed to this heat and humidity. When we've had tea, would you unpack my things for me? Then I'll go and lie down for an hour.'

'Of course. Shall I do it now? Then your room will be ready as soon as you've had tea. I can have my *refresco* later, and I expect you'd like to talk to Raul as he's leaving tomorrow.'

'Very well ... here are my keys. You'll have to use your common sense about where to put things.'

'Our rooms are on the upper level,' said Raul, with a gesture at the balcony above the cloister-like walkway at ground-floor level. 'We're next door to each other and our luggage has been taken up.' He handed her two of the three keys he was holding.

As she hurried away, she heard his aunt say, 'That was tactful of the child.'

She said something else but by then Maria was too far away to overhear. Perhaps it was not surprising that Miss Dysart should see her as a child, but it reinforced Maria's resolve to look as grown up as possible at dinner this evening.

Having mounted the stairs to the upper walkway, she had to go round to the other side of the patio to come to the rooms allotted to them. Looking over the balustrade, she could see a waiter serving tea to the others. Raul was sitting sideways on the banquette, his arm stretched along the top of the backrest behind his aunt's shoulders. Today he wasn't wearing a *guayabera* but a short-sleeved shirt of striped cotton, the edge of the sleeve bisecting the part of his upper arm where a well-developed muscle showed when he lifted things. While she was looking down at him, he glanced upwards, saw her and raised his forearm in a friendly wave. She found herself wishing he wasn't going away tomorrow but was spending the whole tour with them.

Wondering what their official driver would be like, she unlocked a door and entered a short passageway with a basin and shower on one side and two yellow-tiled alcoves on the other. In these were Miss Dysart's cases.

The room opening out from the end of the passage had two built-in single beds covered with thick scarlet cotton. There was also a built-in bench with cushions of pink-striped beige cotton to match the heavy curtain. A large window overlooked the hotel's outer garden.

She had unpacked the smaller case and was starting to hang up the dresses and skirts in the larger one when someone tapped at the door. Expecting to open it to a member of the hotel staff, Maria was surprised to find Raul outside. He was carrying a tall glass of fruit juice with a slice of orange and some greenery hooked on the rim.

'I thought you might be thirsty,' he said. 'And that you might not know how to adjust the air-conditioning.'

As she thanked him for the drink, Maria wondered if it had been his idea or his aunt's. She took a refreshing sip while he fiddled with the controls at the side of a ventilation unit high up on the outer wall which she hadn't noticed before. A few seconds later there was a whirring noise and she felt the warmth of the room beginning to cool down.

'Personally I prefer open windows and an overhead fan, but the humidity doesn't bother me,' said Raul. 'How are you getting on? Can you manage?'

'Yes, thank you.'

In fact she was enjoying her task. Miss Dysart's clothes were a revelation. Maria hadn't known that elderly ladies wore diaphanous nightgowns with billowing robes to match and finest lawn undergarments pin-tucked and edged with lace. Both the silk dresses were labelled 'Céline—Paris' at the back of the neck. She knew they were silk because she had seen another label, 'soie', discreetly stitched to a side-seam.

'Your great-aunt has beautiful clothes.'

He smiled. 'Clothes are one of her pleasures. She enjoys dressing up in the evening. But as long as you're neat and clean, that's all that matters. These places are very informal. Most tourists don't bring many clothes. I'm going to have a swim. When you've finished here, come and join me. I'll pick up a pool towel for you. They don't like the room towels being used.'

He went out, closing the door behind him.

Maria had smoothed all the sheets of white tissue paper used by whoever had packed for Miss Dysart, and had closed the cases and put them out of the way when there was another knock.

'Raul's in the pool, where I'm sure you'd like to be,' said his aunt, as she entered. 'What is the room like?'

'I think it's very nice...but I've never stayed in an expensive hotel before,' said Maria.

Miss Dysart inspected her quarters. 'Hmm...a bit on the poky side but the bed feels comfortable,' she said, after prodding one. 'Thank you for unpacking for me. Off you go. I'll see you at dinner.'

Maria's room was the same as Miss Dysart's but reversed. It took her less than ten minutes to arrange her belongings and have a quick shower to clean herself before going down to the pool. Drying with one of the densely piled bath towels might be a commonplace experience to the others. To her it was the height of luxury.

Miss Dysart's swimsuit had been made in the USA. It had a skirt and, inside, a type of bra, as well as a matching wrap. Maria had nothing to cover her own bathing suit. It had been a present from her father on her sixteenth birthday and the fabric, originally black, had discoloured and lost its elasticity. She hoped people wouldn't stare at her, amazed at anyone wearing such a shabby garment. She hadn't liked to suggest buying a new one in addition to all the other new things she had needed: the shoes, three new pairs of briefs, a sponge-bag and other essentials.

Leaving her room, she heard a splash from below and looked over the balustrade to see a long brown shape gliding under the water towards the opposite side where the fronds of a tall palm tree cast flickering shadows on the floor of the pool.

When Raul broke the surface, water streaming from powerful shoulders, she could see, as soon as he stood up, that it wasn't very deep.

After a moment's pause to rake back his thick black hair, he bent at the knees and propelled himself lazily backwards until, in the middle of the pool, he clasped his hands under his head, crossed his legs at the ankle, and lay with closed eyes, floating, as if he were lying in a hammock.

Maria watched him, aware of peculiar sensations aroused by his athletic body. He was not the first man she had seen wearing only a brief bathing slip but she couldn't remember ever before wanting to imprint the image on her memory so that it would always be there.

She went down to join him, slipping quietly into the pool so that she wouldn't disturb his train of thought or perhaps a deliberate attempt to clear his mind of all thoughts.

But at that point some other people came for a swim and their loud conversation made Raul raise his head and look round, first at the newcomers and then at Maria treading water.

'There you are.' A couple of strokes brought him alongside. 'I was beginning to think you weren't coming down.'

'I felt rather hot and sticky so I had a quick shower.'

'Our towels are over there on the reclining chairs. This isn't much of a pool, size-wise.' He lowered his voice. 'A few more hippo-sized people like that lot and we'll be shoulder to shoulder.'

Maria glanced at the party of four who had entered the water by way of a wide flight of steps flanked by copies of ancient statues. All the newcomers were massively overweight and the pallor of their skin suggested that this time yesterday they had been somewhere much colder.

She said, 'I think it's a lovely pool... like an oasis. It was clever to leave that big old tree growing over there when the patio was built. Whoever designed this hotel had a lot of good ideas. I like all the glassed-in recesses displaying bits of ancient pottery in the walls of the corridors.' A thought struck her. 'It wasn't you, was it? The first time we met you said you had studied architecture and were involved in the new resort south of Playa.'

He shook his head. 'I had nothing to do with this place. The public spaces are good but, in my view, the rooms are too small. However it's the best accommodation at Cobá.'

'Perhaps they seem small to you because you're so tall,' said Maria, flinching slightly as loud cackles of laughter were amplified by the patio's acoustics.

'Let's go and sunbathe,' said Raul. 'The sun will be setting before long.'

Instead of swimming to the steps, he placed the flat of his hands on the edge of the pool and, with one fluid moment which flexed all the muscles under his smooth bronze skin, lifted himself out. Then he reached down to help her.

Maria didn't need assistance. Her arms were slender but strong and it would have been no problem to hoist herself out. Oddly reluctant to take the strong hand offered to her, she put hers up to meet it and found herself grasped not by the hand but by her wrist. The next moment she was standing beside him.

'What are you made of? Fibreglass? You weigh next to nothing,' he said.

'I'm not that skinny,' Maria retorted defensively.

'Just fine-boned, hmm?' he said, smiling.

Embarrassed by her ratty old suit and by his amused appraisal of the body inside it, she turned away, glad, a few moments later, to envelop herself in one of the man-sized pool towels.

Raul rough-towelled his head before raking back his hair with the same casual gesture he had used in the pool.

'Would you like another fruit drink?'

She would, but she had the feeling that, with all that fancy decoration, they had to be expensive. She shrank from being thought to be what her father called a freeloader.

'Not at the moment, thank you. What time is dinner?'

'I should think we'll eat about eight. It depends on Aunt Iris. I'll give her a call about seven. She won't like not having a bath to lie in, but that can't be helped.'

'They're lovely showers. I'm not used to hot water. Or even much fresh water. My father has rigged up a spray for rinsing my hair, but we have to be careful with water. We never waste it.'

'You needn't economise here. Have as many showers as you like. Wash your hair twice a day.' He stretched his long frame on a lounger. 'It's a Robinson Crusoe-Girl Friday kind of life your father imposes on you, isn't it?'

In the act of reclining, she sat up with a jerk. 'He doesn't impose it on me. I like it... it's a good life.'

'But you've never known anything else.'

'I've read books. I know something about the way other people live. They aren't necessarily happier than we are.'

'No, they aren't,' he agreed. 'And a lot of them don't have much choice in the way they live either. But I think your options are unnecessarily limited. By arranging his life the way he wants it, your father is stopping you from making the most of yours.'

'That isn't true,' she said angrily, but keeping her voice low. 'If you're born with a gift, like my father, you have a duty to protect it... nurture it. He needs to be where he is. He couldn't work in a city.'

'Maybe not... but having a daughter is also a duty. Every child has the right to be properly educated. By now you should be at a university or technical college.'

The fact that he might be right didn't stop her saying fiercely, 'I don't want to be one of those tough career-women battling my way to the top of some giant corporation. It doesn't appeal to me.'

'Would you like to a be a nun?'

She was taken aback. Could he seriously think she might have a religious vocation?

'No, I shouldn't like that life either.'

'It's the way you seem to be heading. Your contacts with the outer world are only slightly less restricted than if you were a novice in one of the enclosed orders.'

'I'm in the outer world now. Father didn't stop me coming here.'

'There were times when I thought he would,' Raul said drily. 'He didn't want to let you go.'

The spur of anger sparked by his critical, judgemental comments died down at the thought of her father spending the evening alone. Was he missing her? Was he lonely?

'I hope he's all right,' she said aloud.

'He'll be fine. I should think he was older than I am when you were born. He got by then. Why not now?'

'He was forty when they had me. Now he's nearly sixty, and not very well.'

'What's the problem?'

'I'm not sure. He won't talk about his health. But he's thinner and always looks tired.'

At that moment a willowy figure in a scarlet bikini walked past them towards the pool where, from the top of the steps, she dipped a toe in the water. A delicious scent lingered on the air behind her. She was wearing a thin gold chain round one shapely ankle. A thicker chain showed at her nape below the glossy blonde hair swept up and held by a red clasp shaped like two hearts with a diamanté arrow through them.

She was carrying one of the blue pool towels. But instead of putting it aside and stepping down into the water she changed her mind and turned round, revealing a pretty face enhanced by skilful eye make-up and a lipstick to match her bikini.

After a brief glance at Maria, her gaze shifted to Raul and then to the three unoccupied loungers beside him.

'Is anyone sitting there?' she asked, in French.

'They're all yours, *mademoiselle*,' he replied, in the same language.

'Thank you.' She spread her towel on the centre one. 'What a beautiful evening. It was so cold when I left Paris. You're very tanned. You must be at the end of your holiday.'

Maria might not know much, but she knew when she was *de trop*. She said quietly, 'Excuse me, I'm going to my room.'

By the time she reached the upper corridor, Raul was sitting up on the centre section of his lounger, facing the pretty Parisienne and laughing at something she had said to him.

CHAPTER THREE

THEY were still there, half an hour later, when she emerged from her room. But now they both had drinks in their hands. The French girl had a straw in her tall glass which was decorated with a flower, and Raul was holding a shorter glass. The girl seemed to be doing most of the talking, illustrating her conversation with graphic gestures and shrugs of her creamy shoulders which no doubt were protected from the sun by some expensive tanning lotion.

Having washed her hair and given it a long rinse under the powerful spray of warm water, Maria intended to find somewhere to sit by the lake in front of the hotel. The patio would soon be in shadow but outside the building the sunlight would last for another half-hour. Once her front hair was dry, she would twist the rest into a coil and fasten it with the beautiful tortoiseshell combs which had belonged to her mother.

There was a small stilt-legged, thatched gazebo jutting out over the water from the lakeshore. No one else was there, except a great many fish who seemed to be crowding round as if they expected her to throw food to them.

Presently the peace of early evening was disturbed by the arrival of a coachload of tourists whose voices, as they disembarked, seemed unnecessarily loud to her. Her reaction to the noise reminded her of Raul's comment that her life had been almost as sequestered as that of a novice.

She wondered if he would invite the Parisienne to join them for dinner. Would a young woman of that age, especially one with her looks, be here on her own? It seemed unlikely. But if she were travelling with a man, where had he been when she came down to the pool? Perhaps she was here with her parents who, like Miss Dysart, were resting.

As the sun sank towards the tree-tops of the jungle on the far bank of the lake, Maria re-entered the hotel. On the far side of the smaller patio a shop had opened for the sale of postcards and souvenirs.

She said to the girl behind the counter, 'Do you sell lipsticks?'

'No, I'm sorry, we have no cosmetics.'

'It doesn't matter.' Maria was leaving the shop, when someone said,

'Excuse me...' Turning, she found a girl of about her own age smiling at her.

'I heard you asking for lipstick,' she said. 'If you've lost your make-up in transit, or left it behind, maybe I can help. I bought some skin cream in the Duty Free shop at Gatwick Airport and they gave me a pack of free samples, including a lipstick. It's not a colour I ever wear but it might suit you. You're welcome to have it, if you'd like to.'

'That's very kind of you,' said Maria.

'Come to my room. I'll give it to you,' said the girl.

On the way to her room, she explained that she and her boyfriend were members of the coach party. She insisted on giving Maria all the free samples. As well as the lipstick, there was a miniature eye-shadow palette, mascara and a tiny bottle of scent.

Maria went back to her own room feeling as if she had just had an encounter with a fairy godmother. The first thing she tried out was the scent. It was called Trésor and, when she rubbed a little on her wrist, it smelt delicious. The eye-shadow was like the golden lights in an abalone shell. Using the applicator, she brushed a little on her lids. Then she used the mascara on the tips of her lashes. The finishing touch was the lipstick. When she sat back to study the effect, it was gratifying to find that she looked considerably older than she had before and not at all like a girl who was going to be a nun.

She was waiting in the corridor when, shortly before eight o'clock, Miss Dysart came out of her bedroom.

'You're looking very nice, Maria. What a charming dress,' she said approvingly.

She herself was wearing a white silk blouse and a black skirt with several ropes of silver beads and long silver earrings.

Maria flushed with pleasure. The white cotton *huipil* with its embroidered yoke and more embroidery at the hem had taken a long time to make. Instead of the multicoloured flowers common to most traditional dresses, she had used only shades of violet, with bows of violet ribbon added to the sleeves.

'I had a most refreshing sleep. What have you been doing?' asked Miss Dysart.

'I swam with Raul and then I made friends with an English girl.'

Miss Dysart looked over the balustrade. 'Raul is down there waiting for us. But first I want to have a look at all these interesting things displayed in the alcoves.'

At night the walkways were lit by concealed wall lights and by the illuminated showcases of ancient pottery. The pool had underwater lights, and there were also green lights hidden among the creepers and shrubs. The effect, to Maria, was magical, although perhaps to people like

Raul and his great-aunt it did not seem as dramatically beautiful as it did to her.

When they arrived on the patio, Raul was chatting, in German, to a middle-aged couple. On seeing Miss Dysart approaching, he excused himself.

'You remembered to use your mosquito repellent, I hope?' he said, coming over to her.

'Yes...on my ankles and wrists. What about you, Maria? Your bare arms are particularly vulnerable.'

'I've put on some lotion,' said Maria. 'But mosquitoes don't seem to like me. I'm almost never bitten.'

'How odd...but what an advantage,' said Miss Dysart. She turned to look up at her nephew. 'I wouldn't mind a short stroll before we have dinner. Is that possible?'

'Of course, but the road outside has some potholes and isn't as well lit as it might be. I'll fetch a flashlight. I won't be long.'

He went off to his room. Tonight he was wearing a well-cut white linen jacket with an open-necked shirt and light blue jeans.

To her disappointment, he didn't seem to have noticed Maria's dress or any change in her appearance.

'Presumably a tie is not *de rigueur* in the dining-room here,' said Miss Dysart. 'How Victorian travellers stood this humidity in their most unsuitable clothes is beyond me. I suppose you hardly notice the heat, having grown up in this climate.'

'I find it much warmer here than where we live, by the sea,' said Maria.

When Raul came back with a torch, he said, 'By the way, there's a room here which doubles as a library and video theatre. I noticed some interesting books on the Mayas which you might like to look at tomorrow, Aunt Iris.'

'When shall we see you again?' she asked.

'I'm not sure. Probably when you reach Mérida...provided I can get away. But you'll be in good hands with Diego. He has excellent recommendations. And I'll leave you a number where you can contact me if necessary.'

'I'm sure we shan't need to do that,' she said, as they left the hotel.

'Would you like to take my arm?' he asked, as they left the well-lit grounds for the darker country road beyond the gateway.

'Thank you.' She tucked her arm through his elbow. 'I do find my night sight isn't as good as it was. Shall we see any wildlife?'

'Most unlikely. If there are any jaguar left in this region, which I doubt, they keep away from the inhabited parts. You'll see turtles in the lake first thing in the morning, if you're up in time. Apart from the ruins, which are closed to the public at dusk, there isn't much here apart from a few shops and restaurants like that little place.'

They were passing a small open-fronted roadside café whose owner had made imaginative use of coloured lighting and egg trays as wall decorations.

'Would it be safe to eat there?' asked Miss Dysart.

'Wherever you eat in Mexico, there's always a chance of being struck down by Montezuma,' Raul said cheerfully. 'Maria is probably immune, but not many visitors escape without at least a mild bout.'

Maria had fallen a few steps behind them. She wondered how she would cope if Miss Dysart should be unwell. It was a responsibility she hadn't foreseen, although she had heard that tourists frequently were taken ill, often from drinks or ice made with unpurified water. There was a notice in the bathrooms here at the Villa Arqueológica saying the tap water was drinkable.

Perhaps there wasn't much to worry about as long as they ate and drank only at expensive places. Miss Dysart was unlikely to want to buy ices or snacks from a street vendor.

Glancing over his shoulder at her, Raul said, 'Maria is used to seeing the stars clearly, but in America and Europe there's too much light pollution for them ever to be seen like this.' He paused to look up at the night sky.

Miss Dysart craned her head backwards. 'Beautiful!' she murmured. 'One would have to lie down to enjoy them to the full. Perhaps after dinner, on one of those chaises-longues in the patio, I might star-gaze for half an hour.'

When they returned to the hotel, the first person they saw, at the far end of the wide corridor leading to the bar, was the young Frenchwoman, now wearing a sleeveless silk top with glittering embroidery on the front, and a pair of flowing white trousers of some filmy material which was lined above the tops of her thighs but showed the rest of her legs.

'Hm . . . a very come-hither outfit,' was Miss Dysart's comment.

'That's Juliette,' said Raul. 'She's from Paris. She's here with her mother and some other French people. Unfortunately all of them except Juliette are under the weather today. She has no English or Spanish. As we all speak French, shall we ask her to have a drink with us?'

'If you wish,' said his aunt.

If Raul sensed her lack of enthusiasm for this suggestion, he chose to ignore it. Lengthening his stride, he strode ahead of them to where the French girl was looking at a travel poster. Maria saw her expression brighten as she turned to him. A few moments later he had his hand on her elbow and was bringing her to meet his aunt.

Miss Dysart replaced her coffee-cup on its saucer, touched her lips with her napkin and, instead of putting it back on her lap, placed it on the table in front of her.

Speaking French, as she had throughout dinner, she said, 'I have still not completely adjusted to the time change so I'm going to leave you young people and go to bed.' As she rose and as Raul and Maria rose with her, she added, 'No doubt you'll breakfast earlier than I shall, Raul. Come and say *au revoir* before you go.'

'Of course. Goodnight, Aunt Iris.'

'Is there anything I can do for you, Miss Dysart?' Maria asked.

'No, thank you, child. Goodnight. Goodnight, *mademoiselle*.'

Her inclination of the head to Juliette, still in her chair, was noticeably cool. A few minutes earlier, without asking if anyone minded, the French girl had lit a cigarette. Maria sensed that this breach of good manners had been all that was needed to clinch Miss Dysart's disapproval of her.

'I think I'll go to bed too,' Maria said, pushing her chair close to the table.

'It's a little early for you, isn't it?' said Raul.

'I'm used to early nights.'

'Did you bring something to read in case you can't sleep?'

'No, but I'm sure I shall sleep. Goodnight,' she said, smiling at Juliette, who responded with an offhand nod.

In the corridor Maria caught up with Miss Dysart who was lingering to study prints of early nineteenth-century drawings made when the cities lost in the jungle were being rediscovered.

Together they toured the ground-floor walkway, looking at the showcases there, and then Miss Dysart remembered her intention to view the night sky from one of the sun-beds on the patio.

'Magnificent!' she murmured, as they lay side by side by the still surface of the swimming-pool, their view of the myriad stars framed by the fronds of the palms growing round the courtyard.

A few minutes after they had said a final goodnight outside their bedrooms, and as Maria was taking the combs from her hair, there was a light knock on the door.

'Raul!' she exclaimed, on opening it.

'I asked the desk if they had any reading matter left behind by other guests,' he said, offering her a bunch of magazines topped by a couple of paperbacks. 'If you've always slept in a hammock, you could find it takes a few nights to adjust to a bed.'

Surprised and touched by his thoughtfulness, she said, 'How kind of you. Thank you.'

'Goodnight.' He was turning away, when he checked, saying, 'By the way, that's a charming dress, but the hairstyle is too sophisticated for you at present. Don't try to run before you can walk, Maria.' Lightly touching her cheek with his forefinger, he repeated his, 'Goodnight,' and walked away in the opposite direction from his room, presumably to rejoin Juliette.

He had been right in thinking she would find it difficult to sleep. The bed felt as hard as a rock compared with the yielding meshes of her hammock; and, unlike a hammock, a bed couldn't be made to swing gently in the manner of a cradle.

By piling up the cushions belonging to the painted concrete banquette which doubled as a bedside table, she was able to arrange herself in a similar position to the one in which she read at home. But no sooner had she settled down to look through the magazines than she realised the air conditioning was making the room too cool for comfort, and the noise of it drove her mad. She jumped up and switched it off, but without achieving full silence because the drone of all the other air conditioners was as loud but not as soothing as the sound she was used to at night, the sea washing over the sand.

The magazines Raul had brought her were a French one called *Madame Figaro*, a German publication and *Bazaar* published in America. With their insights into lifestyles very different from her own, they kept her absorbed for more than an hour.

Eventually she fell asleep with the light on, only to wake with a start when *Bazaar* slid to the floor.

I must learn to sleep like other people, she thought, putting the cushions back where they belonged and stretching out on the mattress. But as soon as she switched off the light, the room became as dark as a deep cave. She had forgotten to open the curtains which were backed with some thick rubbery material, presumably to blot out the sun during the day. There was also a lace curtain to prevent people crossing the garden from seeing into the room. This she also drew aside. The window itself was a single large pane sealed into place. There was no way of letting in air except by means of the noisy machine in the wall.

'Maria!'

She woke up, with a startled jerk, to find Raul's hand on her knee and his face on a level with hers as he crouched on his haunches in front of the bench by the lake where she was sitting.

She had come out early to watch the turtles poke their heads out of the water as the sun rose. Worn out by a sleepless night, she had nodded off for a few minutes.

'You were just about to topple over,' said Raul, removing his hand. 'I gather your first night on a bed wasn't too successful.'

'No... but I'll get used to it. I found the room a bit claustrophobic.'

'I know what you mean. They're small and the ceilings are low. I felt rather caged myself. You'll prefer tomorrow night's accommodation. At Chichén Itza you'll be staying in a big old house which used to be a *hacienda*.'

He rose and sat down beside her. She caught a faint whiff of a pleasant aroma, either soap or some kind of lotion. His hair was still damp from the shower, his cheeks and chin freshly shaved. She found herself staring at the taut brown skin at his jawline and quickly averted her eyes to where the turtles were beginning their curious early morning display.

Presently Raul glanced at his watch and said, 'I'd better have breakfast.' He rose. 'Will you join me?'

She hesitated. She was longing for a cup of coffee, but perhaps he would really prefer to breakfast alone. Her father was never sociable first thing in the morning. She had learnt long ago not to speak until she was spoken to.

'A glass of freshly squeezed orange juice is an excellent pick-me-up after a restless night,' he said. 'Come on.'

They did not, as she had expected, have the dining-room to themselves. The people who had arrived by coach the previous evening were occupying several tables.

Raul led the way to the table farthest away from the sound of their voices and drew out a chair for Maria.

'Thank you.' As she sat down, she wondered if Juliette would join them or if she was still asleep. At the end of their evening together, had Raul kissed her goodnight? After dark the patio offered a number of shadowy corners where two people could embrace. It was even possible that he had been to the French girl's room ... spent part of the night there. Maria knew such things happened. Deploring the lax morals of the present generation compared with the strict supervision given to girls in her mother's day was one of her father's most frequently repeated diatribes.

She found the idea of Raul making love to Juliette curiously repugnant. Her thoughts must have shown in her expression, for he said, 'What's the matter? Are you feeling queasy?'

'Oh, no ... I feel fine,' she said hurriedly.

'Good. I'm relying on you to keep a close eye on my aunt. She's inclined to forget that she's not as young as she was. Don't let her overdo it.'

'I'll try, but how do I restrain her without sounding impertinent?'

'Exercise your tact,' said Raul.

At which point the waiter came to take their orders for breakfast.

By the time Miss Dysart and Maria returned to the hotel for lunch, their driver and guide, Diego, had arrived. But he did not eat with them. After lunch, Miss Dysart said she would rest for an hour, returning to the ruins in the forest later.

When Maria went for a swim there was no one about but the maids busy cleaning the bedrooms in readiness for a new intake of guests. It seemed that most of the tourists spent only one night at Cobá. Miss Dysart's itinerary allowed for at least two nights at each of the sites they were visiting, longer if she chose to linger.

Maria was sitting on the edge of the pool, dangling her feet in the water and wondering when they would see Raul again, when someone said, 'Hello,' and she looked up to see a young man with a pack on his back smiling at her from the opposite side of the pool.

He looked in his early twenties and was wearing trainers, shorts and a T-shirt which wouldn't stand up to many more washings. His hair was damp with the sweat which glistened on his face and arms. He looked as if he had walked a long way in the hottest part of the day.

'Hello,' she said, smiling back at him.

'You look nice and cool. I can't wait to get in the pool, but I'd better wash up first. See you.' With a flip of the hand, he went off to find his room.

She watched him go, wondering about his nationality. He had blue eyes and sounded from north of the border but there was another accent mixed with the American one. It surprised her that a back-packer could afford to stay at an expensive hotel like the Villa Arqueológica; perhaps there wasn't any cheaper accommodation at Cobá.

She was swimming when he reappeared in a very brief bright green slip. His physique was slight compared with Raul's, but he looked fit and held himself well. He entered the pool by taking a shallow header from the edge and swimming to where Maria was treading water.

'Hello again. My name is Chris, short for Christian. I'm from Denmark.'

'I'm Maria... from here in Mexico.'

He looked surprised. 'I thought maybe you were from my part of the world.'

'My great-grandparents were from Norway. I've never been to Europe. Have you just arrived in Mexico?'

'I was in Mexico City for a couple of weeks before flying to Cancún. Now I'm working my way round the peninsula before going to Guatemala. I don't usually stay in places like this but once in a while I treat myself to the luxury of a bed.'

'You speak perfect English.'

He grinned. 'It's necessary. Not many people speak Danish. My Spanish is not so good, but it's improving every day. Do you work for Club Med or are you also a tourist?'

'I'm here to interpret for an English visitor. She's resting at the moment.'

'Is that your job...interpreting for foreigners?'

'This is the first time I've done it. Normally I keep house for my father. He's an artist. We live on the Caribbean coast. Do you have a job or are you a student?'

'I'm a freelance journalist,' said Christian. 'My family have been in the newspaper business for a long time. I worked as a reporter until I had saved enough money to spend a year travelling. I want to be a travel writer but I don't know if I'm good enough to make a living. At the end of the year I may have to go back to Denmark and settle down. My father wants me to take his place when he retires. But he's not fifty yet and I have a sister who will be joining the paper when she finishes her studies at the university in Copenhagen. She may want to take over from him. Do you have brothers and sisters?'

Maria shook her head. 'My mother died when I was a baby. It must be nice being part of a big family.'

'Sometimes. I like my family, but I meet a lot of people who don't get along with theirs or whose parents have split up. If the bar's open, I'm going to buy a bottle of water to replace all the sweat I've lost today. Would you like a beer or an orange juice?'

It sounded as if he couldn't really afford to stand other people drinks. Maria said, 'Not right now, thank you.'

He was nice, she thought, as he swam off towards the steps. Quite different from Raul. Not as sure of himself, not as worldly. Already she felt comfortable with him.

The pool had a ledge shaded by the thatch of the *palapa*. When he came back they sat there and continued chatting while he drank a litre of mineral water. He wanted to know all about her and her father and Miss Dysart. Either by nature or training he was extremely inquisitive, but his curiosity was warming rather than intrusive.

They were still there when Miss Dysart leaned over the wall behind them and said, 'The place seems deserted. Will you find someone and order tea, please, Maria.'

'Of course. I'm sorry... I didn't realise what the time was.'

Christian scrambled to his feet on the ledge. 'Good afternoon, ma'am. I'm Christian Eriksen.'

'How do you do?' said Miss Dysart, shaking the hand he offered. 'I am Iris Dysart. Will you take tea with us? Or perhaps you'd rather have a cold beer?'

The invitation surprised Maria, who had thought her employer might be annoyed at finding her chatting to a stranger instead of being dressed and ready to perform any services required of her. But Miss Dysart's expression was much more affable than it had been last night when Raul presented Juliette to her.

'It's kind of you, ma'am, but it's time I dressed and went to see the ruins. I only got in about an hour ago. It was nice to find someone to talk to while I was cooling off. Excuse me.'

Ten minutes later, when tea had been ordered and Maria had been up to her room to dress, Miss Dysart said, 'Is that young man an American?'

'He's a Dane.'

'So his name suggests, but his accent and his way of addressing me as "ma'am" made me think his family might have emigrated. An admirable nation, the Danes. They once ruled England, you know. King Canute was a Dane. But I dare say you've never heard of him.'

When Maria said she had, and produced some facts to prove it, her employer said, 'You astonish me. Although they've all been to good schools, I doubt if my great-nieces and their friends have heard of him. Their general knowledge is lamentable. Yours is excellent. You have yet to give me that blank look which is so often the reaction of your generation of my family to some commonplace reference.'

Her praise made Maria glow. Perhaps the hours spent poring over the encyclopaedia had been well spent after all.

That evening, they were having a drink in the bar before dinner, when a waiter came to find them with a message for Maria to translate.

'Raul is on the telephone, Miss Dysart.'

'You had better come with me. He may want a word with you.'

The waiter led them to a telephone. After the switchboard had made the connection, Miss Dysart listened for a moment before saying, 'A most interesting day and everything has gone smoothly. I find Diego perfectly satisfactory. Another coach party has replaced last night's influx. The new lot are German-speaking Swiss tourists. There are also some independent travellers including a very nice Dane. Christian Eriksen. I'm going to ask him to dine with us.' She paused. 'No, not my generation. A boy in his twenties. Maria made friends with him in the pool this afternoon and we saw him again on our second visit to the ruins.'

After some more conversation, she said, 'Yes, she's here. I'll put her on. Goodnight, my dear.'

She handed the receiver to Maria who put it to her ear. 'Hello?'

'You've made a new friend, I hear.' The distinctive timbre of Raul's voice was emphasised by the telephone.

'He's a journalist. Talking to people is part of his job.'

'How's your job going? Any problems?'

'Not so far.'

At this point Miss Dysart signalled that she was returning to the bar.

'What did you think of the ruins?' Raul asked, while his aunt was walking away. 'Were they up to your expectations?'

'Wonderful. This afternoon we climbed the tallest pyramid. It's only when you can see over the jungle that you realise what a huge city Cobá was. Diego told us the restoration has come to a standstill for lack of money.'

'Did he climb the pyramid with you?'

'No, he stayed with Miss Dysart. I went up with Chris. Your aunt asked him to take some snaps with her camera for her.' As Miss Dysart was now out of earshot, she added, 'It's a shame she suffers from vertigo and can't see the views for herself.'

'Even without climbing steps, it's a steam bath in there. Make sure she drinks plenty of water. You too. Goodnight.'

'Goodnight, Raul.' She replaced the receiver.

He had sounded rather brusque. Perhaps he had had a difficult day.

* * *

The next morning, after breakfast, they set out for Chichén Itzá. Having discovered that this was also the next place on Chris's itinerary, Miss Dysart offered him a lift which he was delighted to accept.

They travelled on an almost deserted motorway through a uninteresting landscape of dense but low-growing vegetation. Diego explained that while Cobá had been overgrown by rainforest, this part of the country, having less rain and less topsoil, was classified as deciduous jungle.

To break the monotony, here and there along the central reservation piles of large rocks had been dumped and sprayed with vivid paint. They saw very few other vehicles, one being a lorry which had overturned, tipping hundreds of fish on to the ground.

'What a waste! I wonder if the driver fell asleep. I can hardly keep awake. I hope Diego doesn't nod off,' said Miss Dysart.

She closed her eyes. Presently her head sank forward on to her chest.

Maria felt sleepy too. Her second night on a bed had been better than the first, and the car was kept cool by air-conditioning, but driving along a straight, flat road with no changes of scenery and no villages to enliven the journey was enough to make anyone drowsy. Considering what the motorway must have cost, and how few motorists were using it, it seemed a terrible waste of money when children like Julio were not being properly educated.

In the front passenger seat, Christian was listening to Diego's life story. From time to time he asked a question. His Spanish was good, but it was the Spanish of Spain, spoken with the lisped 'c' which in Mexico was considered an affectation.

Although George Rawlings claimed that his wife's family were descended from the conquistadores who had discovered this part of the New World in the sixteenth century, secretly Maria felt that such a heritage carried more shame than pride with it. She had always identified with the conquered rather than the conquerors. She wondered what Chris thought about it. There was little doubt whose side Raul would be on. It did not require much imagination to see his aquiline features on the bridge of a galleon or commanding an attack.

She was woken from a dream about him by a touch on her wrist. It was Christian, reaching between the front seats to alert her to the fact that they were nearly there.

That afternoon, while Miss Dysart was having her nap and Maria and Christian were sitting on the edge of the huge pool at the Hotel Hacienda Chichén, he said, 'When I woke you up in the car, when we arrived here, for a moment you looked frightened. Had you been having a bad dream?'

'I expect my subconscious is disturbed by all this excitement,' she said lightly. 'I'm not used to travelling like you are.'

'What were you dreaming?' he persisted.

'I've forgotten,' she said evasively. 'It was very confused. It didn't make sense when I woke up.'

But in fact the dream was still clear and vivid in her mind. It had followed on from her thoughts before she fell asleep. She had dreamt that Raul had been one of the Spanish commanders and she had been one of a group of prisoners. The others had been sentenced to death, but she had been spared and taken to his private quarters. When she had understood the reason for her selection, she had begged him to spare her. But he had been adamant. She must either submit to him or die with the others. At which point Chris had woken her.

'Do you dream in Spanish or English?' he asked.

'At home I don't often have dreams. What time is it, Chris?'

He was wearing a waterproof watch. Holding his left wrist towards her, he said, 'Nearly time for Miss Dysart's afternoon tea. I'd better go back to my place. Perhaps I'll see you later, at the ruins. I wish I could afford to stay here, but it's way above my budget.'

Originally the hotel had been a *hacienda*, the great house of a large estate. But its chief claim to fame was as the home of an American consul, Edward Thompson, who had spent much of his time in the Yucatán, studying and writing about the Mayas.

Chris was spending the night at another Villa Arqueológica, a short distance down the road. Maria suspected that staying there was stretching his budget but that he wanted to keep in touch with them, perhaps because he was hoping to be offered a lift to the Mayan remains at Uxmal, the next place on their route.

Or he might enjoy talking to Miss Dysart about her previous travels. She was a good raconteur and had told them many interesting tales at dinner the night before. It wouldn't have been surprising if, later, he had jotted some of them down for possible use in future travel articles.

Maria didn't feel that her company was the reason he was staying near by. Although they were close in age, and she had some Scandinavian blood in her, the restricted nature of her life must make her a boring companion compared with most of the girls he met. True, she had made many so-called armchair journeys, but that wasn't the same as having real life adventures. Chris had already been to most of the countries in Europe as well as travelling from coast to coast in the United States before coming to Mexico.

They did meet at the ruins later and Miss Dysart again invited him to dine with them.

'It's good for you to mix with your contemporaries,' she remarked, when they were waiting for him to arrive. 'It sounds to me as if you haven't had enough young companionship.'

They dined on the lofty veranda at the back of the *hacienda* attended by two elderly waiters. The diners were elderly, too. Maria noticed that the American couple at the next table spoke only to the waiters, either because they were exhausted from sight-seeing or had nothing to say to each other. She might not have noticed them but for the fact that the wife was wearing the most beautiful blouse Maria had ever seen.

When she asked Miss Dysart what it was made of, the Englishwoman said, 'That is lawn, a very fine cotton or linen, and I should think it was made in Italy, one of the last places where that exquisite hand embroidery is still done, mainly by nuns.'

After dinner, Miss Dysart said she was going to read in bed. Chris asked her permission to take Maria to his hotel where a video about Chichén Itza was to be screened at ten o'clock.

'By all means, as long as you walk back with her afterwards. I know it's not far but I would rather she didn't come by herself.'

'I wouldn't let her do that, ma'am.' He sounded faintly indignant that she could suppose he would.

'In that case, I'll say goodnight.'

As Miss Dysart was turning away, Maria said, 'Raul hasn't telephoned yet.'

'I don't expect him to ring up every night. If he were going to, he would have done so by now.'

The Villa Arqueológica down the road was almost identical to the one they had left and although it was not as romantic as the *hacienda* surrounded by magnificent trees, a much younger and livelier bunch of guests was crowding the bar and waiting to see the video.

Afterwards Chris persuaded her to stay for another drink—beer for him, papaya juice for her—and then he escorted her back.

It was a bright moonlit night and he didn't need to use his flashlight. A few yards inside the gates of the *hacienda*, the drive was crossed by a narrow-gauge railway track.

'Diego says this line was laid for mule-drawn trucks to transport loads of sisal,' Maria said, keeping her voice down in case the occupants of a nearby guest cottage should be asleep. 'Sometimes the mules pulled coaches taking the landowners and their families on visits to neighbouring *haciendas*.'

At the junction with the path to the cottage where she and Miss Dysart were staying, Chris said, 'I'll leave you now. I'll be at the ruins all day tomorrow so I'm sure to see you. Goodnight, Maria. Sleep well.'

He bent and kissed her cheek before walking away at a brisker pace than before.

It was the first time a man had kissed her and, although it had been more friendly than romantic, it made her heart flutter slightly as she watched him hurry away. It crossed her mind that he might be going at that speed because he had wanted to kiss her properly but felt that he shouldn't.

Reluctant to go inside on such a beautiful night, she strolled slowly along the path, looking up through the tracery of branches at the starscape which Raul had said could not be seen as clearly in other parts of the world because of light pollution.

And then, as she neared the cottage, where a lamp was still alight in Miss Dysart's bedroom, she saw that someone was sitting in one of the rocking chairs on the veranda.

For a moment she thought it must be Diego and wondered why he was there. Then the man rose from the chair and she saw it was Raul, which made her heart start to thump in a far more disturbing way than when Chris had kissed her goodnight.

He stepped down from the veranda and came swiftly to where she had come to a startled standstill.

'I've been waiting for you to come back,' he said softly. Then, taking her by the arm, he swung her round and frogmarched her back the way she had come. 'I have things to say to you, my girl.'

CHAPTER FOUR

AT THE great house, four people were having coffee and brandies at one of the tables in the room between the front and rear verandas. Everyone else seemed to have retired for the night.

Still grasping her arm, Raul beckoned the bar waiter and asked for a rum and Coke. He didn't order anything for her.

'We'll be round the corner,' he said, in Spanish. Then he propelled her to some chairs on the front veranda where he said curtly, 'Sit down.'

'Why are you angry?' said Maria, beginning to recover from her initial bewilderment.

'You are not here to make up lost time in the boyfriend department. You're here to look after my aunt,' Raul told her coldly.

Having ordered her to sit down, he remained on his feet.

'But I had her permission to go out,' Maria protested. 'I was only across the road at the Villa Arqueológica. We were watching a video.'

'Which started at ten and lasted under half an hour.' Without looking at his watch, he added, 'It's after eleven.'

'We had a drink and discussed the film afterwards.'

'What sort of drink?'

His inquisitorial manner reminded her of her father. But he wasn't her father. Nor, even if he had arranged this job for her, was he her employer. She was answerable only to Miss Dysart.

80

On the spur of the moment, she said, 'A Tequila Sunrise.'

It was the name of a drink she had often seen chalked on boards outside the tourist bars in Playa del Carmen. She had never had one, although she had once tried an experimental sip of tequila, a spirit distilled from the agave plant.

To her palate the taste was vile. It amazed her that anyone could drink the stuff for pleasure. But Mexican men seemed to like it and her father sometimes drank a glass or two in the evening. And she knew that hundreds of thousands of margaritas, made from tequila and lemon or lime juice with the rim of the glass dipped in salt, were consumed by the people George Rawlings contemptuously called 'the holidaying hordes'.

'Did you enjoy it?' Raul asked.

Foreseeing that if she said yes, he might suspect that she hadn't and take a punitive pleasure in watching her force down another, she said, 'No, I didn't, actually. But I couldn't see any harm in trying one. I'm nineteen . . . not nine, you know.'

'In terms of experience, you're still newly hatched,' said Raul. 'As vulnerable as a chicken which has just scrambled out of its eggshell. Your father consigned you to our care on the understanding that you'd be protected from the hazards you haven't yet learned how to deal with. Unfortunately my aunt's experience of life is also limited in some respects. She equates good manners and clean nails with moral standards that haven't applied for several decades.'

'She saw through Juliette,' said Maria. 'Not that her manners were good. As for moral standards...I shouldn't think she has any.'

Raul's right eyebrow lifted. 'A rather sweeping judgement, don't you think?'

'No more sweeping than your conclusion that Chris is out to seduce me. I did spend some time with Juliette. You haven't even met Chris.'

'No doubt I'll meet him tomorrow. But whether he'll hang around when he finds I've rejoined the party remains to be seen,' Raul said, in a sardonic tone. 'He won't be hitching a lift on the run to Uxmal, if that's what he has in mind. There won't be room for him.'

Maria's reaction to this unexpected announcement was mixed. There hadn't been time to wonder why he had come, or how long he was staying. But as they weren't leaving for Uxmal until the day after tomorrow, he was obviously going to be with them for at least two nights.

'I thought you were busy,' she said. 'That the only reason I was here was because you hadn't the time to accompany Miss Dysart.'

'That was the principal reason. *Gracias*——' This to the barman who had arrived with his drink on a salver on one hand and carrying a small table in the other.

'Perhaps the *señorita* would like a glass of iced water,' the man suggested, presenting Raul with a chit and a pen to sign it.

'Thank you, no. It's past the *señorita's* bedtime and no doubt she'll find some drinking water in her room,' said Raul.

'Of course, *señor*.' The man took back his pen and picked up the chit and his tip. 'Thank you, *señor*.' With a bow for Raul and a smile for Maria, he left them.

'I am *not* a child!' she said fiercely, as soon as he was out of earshot. 'I resent being treated like one.'

At first it seemed Raul was going to ignore this remark. 'Rather a nice little wine table,' he said, as he picked up the tall glass with ice floating in it. 'A genuine antique by the look of it. Possibly imported. Possibly a locally made copy.' He tasted his drink. Then, turning to look at her, he added, 'The charms of antique furniture are one of the many pleasures you have yet to discover.' He crossed his long legs and took another long swallow of the rum and Coke.

Then, just as she had decided to say goodnight and leave him to it, he shot out a hand and closed his fingers round her forearm.

'All right. I'll give you a sample of how I would treat you if you were twenty-five and had had several lovers and were here on your own, looking for an amorous adventure,' he said casually.

The next moment her wrist was pressed to his mouth and there was a gleam in his eyes which made her insides clench in a most disturbing way. When he then slid his fingers up to hold her palm and rub it against the slight roughness of his cheek, she was even more disturbed. And when he then kissed her palm, she experienced a rush of sensations which made her feel as if she had been drinking tequila and if she tried to stand up her legs might not support her.

Raul's fingers slid back to her wrist and moved it so that her elbow was once again resting on the arm of her chair. But he didn't let go.

'So... given that we are in this hypothetical situation, how would you react?' he enquired, his thumb moving gently over the inside of her wrist.

Trying not to show how profoundly his actions had unnerved her, although there was nothing she could do to slow down her racing pulse, Maria said unevenly, 'How did Juliette react?'

'Juliette wasn't given the opportunity. What made you think she might be?'

'It seemed a possibility.'

'On the contrary... an impossibility. You have a lot to learn about men's tastes in women. However, it's late and I've had a long, tiring day. We'll continue this tutorial another time.' He released her arm and stood up. 'Off you go. Goodnight, Maria.'

When Miss Dysart came out of her room the following morning, she found Maria sitting on the veranda, waiting for her.

After saying good morning and making polite enquiries about each other's sleep, they set out for breakfast.

'Raul has come back,' said Miss Dysart. 'He arrived after you had gone out and was rather displeased with me for letting you go. What time did you get back?'

'A bit later than I intended, but not very late. Raul was waiting for me on our veranda. Didn't you know?'

'No, I didn't. After he left my room, I took out my hearing aid.' To Maria's surprise, she put her hand to her ear and extracted a small blob of flesh-coloured plastic. 'Although my new aid is by far the best I've ever had, I don't leave it in all night. Very neat, don't you think?' She put it back in her ear, holding her hair aside for Maria to see how unnoticeable it was. 'My deafness isn't severe. It's just one of the penalties of being old. Was Raul very cross with you?'

'Rather cross, yes.'

Miss Dysart gave a dry chuckle. 'When he was Christian's age, Raul was the type of young man who in my day used to be known as Not Safe In Taxis. I can't speak from experience because I was such a Plain Jane that my virtue—as it was called then—was never under attack. But, from what I have heard and read, young men were ever thus. It's a phase they go through and, generally speaking, grow out of... if they're intelligent. Certainly Raul is long past *his* wild oats phase, and

Christian too, I dare say. Young as he is, he strikes me as serious-minded. A nice boy. I like him extremely.'

Raul had already started his breakfast when they walked through the house to the rear veranda. He rose to draw out a chair for his aunt while a waiter did the same for Maria.

As she sat down and unfolded her napkin, Maria avoided Raul's eye. The effect of last night's 'tutorial' was still potent. She had seen in her first quick glance that his face was now smoothly clean-shaven, but more than nine hours later her palm retained, like a physical imprint, the curiously exciting texture of last night's incipient stubble.

She knew it would be a long time before she forgot that feeling...or the ice-coldness of his lips on her wrist. Those memories would linger long after the bruise he had left above her elbow had faded. She knew he hadn't meant to hurt her and would be embarrassed if she displayed the small blueish marks made by the tips of his fingers biting into her flesh while he marched her away from the cottage.

Yet, later, his touch had been light. Clearly his long brown fingers with their surgically clean nails could be gentle when he chose. The thought of him touching other parts of her body made her mouth go dry, her heart start to hammer. She blanked out the unseemly images, afraid he might read her mind. Then told herself not to be foolish. He thought her too young and pure to have such thoughts. He would never guess she had spent half the night restlessly wondering what it would be like to feel his lips on her mouth, not cold as they had been last night after drinking the iced Cuba Libre but warm...warm and passionate.

Even now, in daylight, in a public place, the thought of being taught to make love by Raul made her insides flutter. When she tried to imagine the same situation with Chris, it was harder to picture and didn't have the same effect. She liked him and found him attractive, but he didn't make her feel the way Raul did...as if she were sharing a branch with a jaguar who wasn't hungry at the moment but who might decide to have her for lunch later on.

'I have some letters to transmit to my office,' said Raul, when he had ordered their breakfasts. 'I'll be busy for about an hour. So I'll join you at the site later, Aunt Iris.'

Miss Dysart said to Maria, 'Raul never goes anywhere without his...modem? Is that right?' When he nodded, she went on, 'You must show it to Maria. It would interest her. When she goes out in the world, she'll need to know about these things. Even I find it fascinating that he can type a letter on his portable computer and a few minutes later his secretary at the Cancún office can print it from her machine and a minute or two after that it can be read in London or New York by means of that other machine whose name I forget.' She looked enquiringly at her great-nephew.

'Fax...short for facsimile.' Raul poured himself some more coffee from his separate pot. To Maria, he added, 'It's one of the many useful gadgets in common use today which, as my aunt says, you'll need to be able to use if you're going to stand on your own feet. Later on I'll show you the small battery-driven computer I take everywhere with me. If we had more time you could learn to type on it, as I did.'

'You may not be aware of it yet, but the world is your oyster, Maria,' said Miss Dysart. 'In my day a girl had to be exceptionally strong-minded to achieve her ambitions if they were in any way unusual. Some women did, but the majority settled for what was expected of them...they married and had children and never developed or even discovered their other capabilities. But your opportunities are limitless.'

'Yes, the sky's the limit for both sexes...*if* they have the get-up-and-go to make their dreams happen,' said Raul. 'But in my observation not many have. It's easier to be a couch potato...someone who sits around watching television,' he added, glancing at Maria. 'What's your ambition? Do you have one?'

'I'd like to travel...see the world.'

'Then there are two options,' he told her. 'Most people with that urge spend fifty weeks a year working wherever they happen to live to pay to go somewhere exotic on their annual vacation. The second option is get a job which involves travelling. The primary qualification for that is to speak more than one language. You're already bilingual in English and Spanish and your French is pretty good. Your looks are another plus. You have a lot going for you. But I wonder if you have the one essential quality?'

'I'm not sure I know what it is.'

He finished his coffee. 'You have to want to be yourself...not George Rawlings' daughter.' He rose from the table. 'I'll see you both later.'

'Raul doesn't mince words,' said Miss Dysart, when they were alone. 'Being a forceful character himself, he hasn't much patience with those of us who lack his drive. I know he thinks it was feeble of me not to assert my independence when I was young. It's my father he takes after. When Raul has daughters he may be despotic too—unless he marries a woman who knows how to keep him in order.'

'Would he stand for being kept in order?' Maria asked doubtfully.

'In my judgement he's the type of man who, if he fell in love, would be very easy to handle. One of the reasons my father became a domestic tyrant was because he didn't love my mother and she irritated rather than soothed him. I realise now that, had I had the courage to stand up to him, he wouldn't have minded,' said Miss Dysart. 'He would have had more respect for me. But often we learn these lessons too late to put them into practice.'

Later, when they returned to their rooms before setting out for the morning's sightseeing, Maria remembered Raul saying, 'Your looks are another plus.' She studied herself in the mirror. Had the compliment been sincere? It didn't seem in character for him to say something he didn't mean. But it didn't necessarily mean that *he* found her attractive.

Yesterday and again this morning she had braided her hair into a single thick plait threaded with a length of blue ribbon. It was less sophisticated than the style Raul had teased her about, but more grown-up than hair hanging loose down her back. She was also wearing lipstick but not eye make-up. As she expected to be climbing the steep steps of the pyramid she had seen in last night's video, she decided to change her skirt for a pair of shorts made from jeans cut off at the knee. To disguise some discoloured and threadbare places, she had sewn on clusters of overlapping multi-coloured patches to look like bunches of balloons attached to chain-stitched strings held in embroidered hands.

An hour later, when she and Chris had climbed the steps to the top of the pyramid called El Castillo, from which the Mayan priests were thought to have hurled sacrificial victims, an American woman said to her, 'I like those Bermudas you're wearing. Did you buy them in the States?'

'Thank you. No, I made them.'

'You mean you copied those cute balloons from a fashion magazine? You don't remember which one it was, do you?'

'They were my own idea.'

'Is that your job... designing resort wear?'

Maria smiled and shook her head, and then the woman's husband called her to pose for a photograph and ended their brief conversation.

When they were back on the ground, Chris wanted to see the temple inside the pyramid not discovered until 1937 and found to contain a jewelled jaguar and a statue of Chac Mool, the Mayan rain god.

However, soon after they entered the dark, narrow passage leading to the heart of the pyramid, Maria began to feel the slimy walls were closing in on her. There was a long line of people shuffling ahead but fortunately no one behind her.

'I'm sorry, Chris, I don't like this. You go on without me. I'm going back outside,' she told him.

To her relief, he didn't try to persuade her, and a few minutes later she was back in the open air recovering from unpleasant sensations which she supposed must have been the onset of claustrophobia.

While she was sitting on a ledge at the base of the pyramid, still feeling slightly queasy from the foetid air in the tunnel, a familiar voice said, 'There you are,' and she opened her eyes to find Raul looming above her.

His expression was stern and she wondered if he had been annoyed at not finding her with his great-aunt. She was about to tell him that it was at Miss Dysart's urging that they'd climbed to the temple of the feathered serpent on top of the pyramid, when he forestalled her.

'Where's your Danish friend?'

'Inside the pyramid. I went a little way in but I had to come out. I know it's silly but I began to feel suffocated.'

'Not silly at all,' said Raul, folding his tall frame into a sitting position beside her. 'I've only been in there once and I didn't enjoy it myself. A pot-holer might not mind the atmosphere in there, but the day I went in someone fainted and several other people panicked. It was no joke getting them out. That's why I was worried about your being in there.'

His concern was warming. It crossed her mind that even the congested tunnel, its walls slimed by thousands of sweaty hands, would be bearable if Raul were with her. It was odd how easily he could undermine her self-possession in some situations, but also give her the feeling that in any kind of emergency or danger she would feel safe with him.

'The last time I came here,' he said, 'was a few years ago at the spring equinox. As Diego has probably told you, the afternoon light creates the illusion that Kukulcán, the feathered serpent, is coming out of his temple and undulating down the side of the pyramid. It's a fantastic feat of architectural engineering and thousands of people come to watch it at both equinoxes. I'm surprised your father has never brought you.'

'He hates crowds,' she said. 'But, except in the tunnel, it doesn't seem crowded at all.' She looked round the wide expanses of grass between the main buildings and was struck by how quiet and empty the place seemed, although in fact there were many groups of visitors listening to their guides explaining its history.

'The guides are adept at not crowding each other,' said Raul. 'Diego is taking Aunt Iris to see the Sacred Well where virgins were sacrificed to the gods. Let's catch them up, shall we? Or do you want to wait for your friend?'

'Chris may be in there some time. He won't expect me to wait.'

Raul rose in a single lithe movement and held out a hand to her. Although it was a very hot day, his fingers and palm felt dry as he pulled her to her feet. His blue and white striped cotton shirt still looked freshly laundered, the unbuttoned collar a crisp frame for the strong brown column of his neck.

Although her hand was in his for only a few moments and he made no attempt to prolong the contact, it was a disturbing reminder of last night's tête-à-tête.

By the time they caught up with the others there was not far to go to the famous *cenote*, a huge sinkhole fed by underground rivers. It was partly surrounded by trees, but with rocks on one side forming natural platforms for the macabre ceremonies which had once taken place there. The surface of the murky water was many feet below the rocks where Diego suggested they should sit while he described what was known of the sacrificial rituals.

'Many valuable ornaments have been recovered,' he told them. 'And more may be hidden in the silt at the bottom of the *cenote*. If it could be drained, the work would be easy. But when they have to work under water, and impeded by trees which have fallen in over the centuries, the archaelogists have many problems.'

Miss Dysart had brought an old-fashioned cream parasol lined with dark green silk to shade her head and shoulders from the sun. Her upright posture with her feet placed neatly together and her free hand spread on one knee made Maria think what a splendid subject for a portrait she would make. *The Spinster*. Or perhaps *An English Eccentric*.

Maria wished she had inherited her father's gift. She was keeping a diary of the trip and would have liked to illustrate it with thumbnail sketches. But she was hopeless at drawing people although she could sketch details of clothes which caught her eye.

Diego's reference to a golden sandal recovered from the *cenote* made her start to visualise the clothes and jewels in which the human sacrifices had been dressed. According to Diego the girls had probably been drugged so that they were scarcely aware of what was happening to them and would have drowned quickly.

Suddenly Raul rose. Speaking Spanish, he said, 'We've had enough gruesome details, Diego. Let's move on to the main Ball Court.'

It was here, in the huge walled court decorated with low-relief carvings of the players of a soccer-type game which had ended with the captain of one side being decapitated by the other captain, that Christian reappeared.

He stood quietly in the background while their guide was talking. Maria wondered if he would introduce himself to Raul or wait for her to introduce them. However it was Miss Dysart who, when Diego had finished, said, 'Raul, this is Christian Eriksen, a Danish journalist we met at Cobá. Raul is the grandson of one of my brothers,' she explained to the younger man.

To Maria's surprise, in view of his attitude the night before, Raul's response to the introduction was friendly.

'What did you think of the jaguar when you finally made the inner chamber?' he asked, after smiling and shaking hands.

Chris shrugged. 'Not much. It's only a copy. The original is in Mexico City.' He turned to Maria. 'You didn't miss anything.'

'It's very hot,' said Miss Dysart, fanning herself with a paper fan attached by a cord to her belt. 'I shall come back later in the day. If you'll walk back with me, Diego, there are some questions I'd like to ask you. Would you care to join us for lunch, Christian?'

'That's very kind of you, ma'am. Thank you.'

'Then I'll see you all at one o'clock.' She and the guide moved off if the direction of the entrance to the grounds.

'Have you seen the *cenote*, Eriksen?' Raul asked.

Chris nodded. 'I went there first but didn't stay long. It's El Caracol, the observatory, that I find the most interesting ruin. The Mayans must have been brilliant mathematicians and astronomers.'

'Forerunners of Tycho Brahe,' said Raul.

Chris looked surprised and pleased. Turning to Maria, he said, 'Tycho Brahe was a Danish astronomer, as famous as Copernicus and Kepler and Galileo, if you've heard of them. You're also interested in astronomy?' he asked Raul.

'I'm more interested in cosmology.'

This remark launched a conversation between the two men to which she listened in silence, slightly miffed by Chris's assumption that the history of astronomy would be a closed book to her.

Presently, Chris said, 'If I'm joining you for lunch, I'd better clean myself up. It was like a Turkish bath in the tunnel. Excuse me.' He loped ahead.

'Were we boring you?' Raul asked. 'Or do you share our curiosity about the origin of the universe?'

If he hadn't added the second question, she would have been tempted to flash back a tart rejoinder. Instead she said lightly, 'I like the early theory... a flat earth draped by a canopy of stars. My father once painted it for me, with galleons and sea monsters falling over the edges and the sky like an old-fashioned curtain draped over a pole, with a full moon in the centre and crescent moons at either end.'

'Do you still have the painting?'

She shook her head. 'He did lots of quick, funny sketches when I was a little girl. I was keeping some of them, but they were destroyed in the hurricane.'

'Tell me about the hurricane?'

His interest surprised her, but at least it was a safe subject, not one which might lead to a continuation of last night's 'tutorial'. Perhaps he had already forgotten his demonstration on the veranda. He seemed to have forgotten his suspicions about Chris.

During lunch the two men found other subjects of mutual interest. It turned out that Chris had an aunt who was an architect, and Raul knew Copenhagen and had friends with a summer house on one of the Danish islands where he had spent sailing holidays.

'These two have a lot in common,' Miss Dysart murmured, in an aside to Maria.

As it turned out, Chris had not been counting on the offer of a lift to Uxmal. He was leaving for their next destination later that afternoon, having persuaded a tour driver to give him an unofficial ride on a coach which was not fully booked.

'Perhaps I'll see you there...or in Mérida,' he said, after thanking Miss Dysart for his lunch.

'We'll look out for you,' she said graciously.

To Maria, he said, 'In case we don't meet again, I've written down my home address. If you ever come to Denmark, I hope you'll call me.' He produced a slip of paper and gave it to her. 'Will you walk to the gate with me?'

As she hesitated, Miss Dysart said, 'Certainly she will, and before I go for my rest I should like another cup of camomile tea, if you please, Raul?'

*   *   *

As they walked down the drive, Chris said, 'I'd like to return Miss Dysart's hospitality, but I can't afford to. Which hotel will you be at in Mérida? Perhaps I could send her some flowers.'

'I'm not sure where we're staying. Do you know where you'll be?'

'The cheapest clean place I can find. I don't think there'll be many expensive hotels in Mérida. It shouldn't be difficult to find you.'

By this time they were near the gateway. 'In case we don't meet again... *buen viaje*,' she said, holding out her hand. 'And if I ever should come to Denmark, I'll call you to say hello.'

'You'll be a welcome guest. Goodbye, Maria.'

Without repeating last night's kiss, he went on his way, looking back from the road to give her a final wave.

Instead of rejoining the others, Maria went to her room. She would have liked to spend Miss Dysart's rest time at the swimming-pool but she thought Raul would be there and, for reasons she could not explain to herself, she felt it was wiser to avoid being with him when his aunt wasn't present.

About ten minutes later she heard footsteps approaching the cottage and Miss Dysart's door opening and closing. After a further ten minutes Maria slipped quietly out and spent the siesta reading on their private veranda.

It wasn't until Miss Dysart emerged, after her nap, that Maria learned she could have swum after all. Soon after lunch Raul had gone back to Cancún by the same means by which he had come. It seemed he had the use of a company helicopter which he flew himself.

'He went in response to an urgent telephone message. He didn't say what had come up, but obviously he felt his presence would be beneficial. He'll come back when the crisis, whatever it may be, is over,' Miss Dysart said comfortably.

Maria felt an irrational sinking of the heart. It would have made more sense to be disappointed by Christian's departure. She was at ease in his company. Whenever Raul was around, she was always on edge.

At Uxmal they spent the night at a Villa Arqueológica almost identical to the one at Cobá. To Maria the Sound and Light performance among the ruins after dark was magical. But after about fifteen minutes Miss Dysart complained of feeling cold and asked Maria to fetch another wrap for her. It was not far to the hotel and Maria was hurrying back when she met Diego helping the Englishwoman to descend a flight of steps leading to the raised terrace where the audience was seated.

'I've seen enough,' said Miss Dysart. 'But by all means stay till the end if you wish to.'

'No, no, I'll come with you,' said Maria, hiding her dismay, in case her employer was feeling unwell and needed looking after.

But it seemed this was not the case for as soon as they returned to the hotel Miss Dysart said goodnight to Diego and led the way to the dining-room.

'I hope you weren't disappointed at not seeing the whole show,' she said, as they waited for their meal to be served. 'You would have been quite safe on your own. For myself, I found the lighting effects becoming repetitive and Diego had already told me that the story of the Mayan princess's love affair was pure fabrication. He disapproves of the history of the Mayas being embellished with nonsense to make it palatable for the more dim-witted tourists.'

Before Maria could reply, an elderly man at the next table turned round and said, 'I agree with that view. I've no doubt Her Majesty the Queen thought the same when the show was first performed in her presence in 1975.'

For a moment Miss Dysart looked disconcerted and even a little put out. But before dinner was over she and her new acquaintance, who introduced himself as Conrad Huntingdon, were conversing as if they had known each other for years.

When Mr Huntingdon invited them to join him for a drink in the bar, and Miss Dysart accepted, Maria asked to be excused as she wanted to write her diary and a letter to her father.

As she had in the room at Cobá, she found the sound of many air-conditioning units, and the stuffy heat of her own room with the unit turned off, made it impossible to sleep.

Eventually the thought of a midnight swim in the pool became overwhelmingly tempting. Minutes later she was out in the fresh air, her bare feet making no sound as she flitted along the pillared corridor of the silent, deserted patio.

She had been swimming for some time, slowly, in order not to make any noise when to her surprise she heard a low murmur of voices coming from the direction of the entrance to the hotel. Moments later two men appeared. One was small and stocky. She recognised him as the porter who had fetched their luggage from the car when they arrived.

Walking behind him, equally unmistakable, was Raul.

CHAPTER FIVE

MARIA froze, hoping that if she stayed motionless she wouldn't be noticed. But the moon was directly overhead and only the corners of the pool were dappled with the breeze-fluttered black shadows of palm fronds and sprays of bougainvillaea.

The spot where she was standing was as brilliantly lit as if a spotlight were beamed on it. A white-skinned tourist in a pale bikini would be less noticeable. But she, golden-brown and wearing her tatty black one-piece, must catch the eye of anyone glancing in her direction.

Too late she realised that, on first hearing the voices, she should have instantly submerged herself and shot across the floor of the pool to lurk, alligator-fashion, by the wall of the *palapa* bar.

It was the Indian who noticed her. He stopped short, his grunt of surprise alerting the tall man behind him. For a moment they both stared at her. Then Raul stepped through the border of plants at the pool's edge and beckoned her to him.

'You should be in bed,' he said softly, when she reached the place where he was standing.

'I couldn't sleep. I'm not doing any harm,' she whispered. Seen from this angle, he looked eight feet tall and the moonlight emphasised the angular structure of his face.

He turned to the porter and gave some low-voiced instructions which, although they were in Spanish, she didn't catch. The man nodded. He was already carrying

Raul's grip. Now, taking charge of his briefcase, he moved on along the corridor.

To her, Raul said tersely, 'Out!'

The peremptory order made her bristle, but she knew she would have to obey it.

By the time she had swum to the steps, he was waiting for her, holding the large blue pool towel she had left there. She gathered her wet hair into a skein and brought it forward to twist out most of the water. As she did so, Raul wrapped the towel round her shoulders.

He did it without touching her, but she was very conscious of his nearness and of the strong brown hands which hadn't touched her.

She dried her arms and her legs before wrapping the towel round her body.

'Where's your key?' he asked, in an undertone.

'I left it in the lock. I've nothing worth stealing. There was no one about. Goodnight.'

As she turned to go, Raul said tersely, 'I want to talk to you.'

'I'm sure it will keep till tomorrow.'

She would have walked away but he said, 'Now, Maria,' and again it was an order.

'We can't go on talking in whispers and our voices will wake people up.'

'I've told the porter to bring us tea in the library.'

'At this hour?'

'Why not? I'm not ready to sleep yet either.' He gestured for her to precede him.

The library was where, the night before last in an almost identical room at Chichén Itza, she had watched a video with Chris. There had been people smoking there, and the odour of stale smoke hung on the air in the library here.

As Raul followed her in, he said, 'We can't sit in this atmosphere. There are chairs down the hall where we shan't disturb anyone.'

There *had* been chairs at Cobá. Here there was a leather-cushioned sofa.

As she sat down, she said, 'What was the point of coming back at this time of night? We're leaving here after breakfast.'

After a slight pause, he said, 'Perhaps I had a pre-monition that you would be doing something foolish.'

'What's foolish about a swim in a hotel pool? It's not like the sea at night.'

'Maybe not, but there are other hazards. Being on your own anywhere at this hour isn't a good idea. Other guests might be wandering about, or one of the staff could get a false impression. There are girls who come on holiday looking for casual affairs.'

'I'm sure there are,' said Maria, thinking of Juliette. 'But does that mean that girls who aren't have to stay behind locked doors all night?' She saw the porter coming with a tray. 'This man, if he'd seen me swimming before you arrived, wouldn't have thought I was one of those people you're talking about.'

'Possibly not. He's an old man. But the night porter might have been young and randy...if you know what that means?'

'Sexually eager or lustful.'

'Your vocabulary seems to be more extensive than I thought. Where did you come across that word?'

'I was looking up Ranelagh in the dictionary and "randy" was just above it.'

While the porter was arranging the tea things on the table in front of the sofa, Raul said, 'When I was a small boy I spent school holidays with my grandmother. She made me read aloud to her for half an hour every day.

Any words I didn't know I had to look up. The next day I'd have to make up a sentence using the words I'd learnt the day before. For example, ''At Ranelagh Gardens in Chelsea, in the eighteenth century, randy young men of fashion went in search of women known as lightskirts.'''

Maria said, 'Why did you stay with your grandmother?'

'Because my father's work took him abroad a great deal and I would have been an encumbrance. My mother died when I was six, but I had two grannies and several aunts. There was no shortage of women in my young life...rather the reverse,' he added drily, before switching to Spanish to thank the porter and sign the chit presented to him.

She wondered if he could remember his mother. It must have been worse to lose her at that age than never to have known her.

But the upsurge of sympathy engendered by a mental picture of small boy bereft of both parents and dependent on the kindness of other relations was abruptly quenched when he said,

'When I hand you over to your father, I'm going to point out that keeping you cloistered with him isn't in your best interests. For a girl of your age to have so little sense of self-protection is ridiculous.'

'I think it's you who's being ridiculous,' Maria said stiffly.

His mention of her father had pricked her conscience. Each day she seemed to spend less time thinking about him, wondering how he was getting on without her. Already at the back of her mind lurked the knowledge that she didn't want to go back to the life they had lived together for so many years. By giving her this taste of freedom, Raul had made it harder for her to accept the

limitations of her real life. For that, and for other reasons
less clear to her, she was suddenly angry with him.

Angry enough to say recklessly, 'How do you know
what I'm really like? Perhaps I've been playing a part.
Perhaps I'm more experienced than you think. My father
goes for long walks. Who knows what I get up to when
he's out of sight up the beach? There are boys of my
age living near us . . . and back-packers wandering past.'

'That may be, but Eriksen was the first to kiss you,
wasn't he?'

'If you say so.'

'I know so. Will you deal with the tea, or shall I?'

The waiter had left several teabags. She dropped one
in each cup and added boiling water. The pool towel,
designed to enfold the most ample tourists, wrapped
round her slim body twice and the double layer at the
back would absorb most of the wetness of her swimsuit.
In any case the sofa had leather squabs which wouldn't
be damaged if some moisture did soak through.

'How was the Sound and Light show?' Raul asked,
as they waited for the tea to be drinkable.

'Wonderful.' She explained why they hadn't seen it
all, adding, 'Miss Dysart wouldn't have minded if I'd
wanted to stay till the end. *She* doesn't fuss over me.'

'She wouldn't approve of your being down here at
this hour. Even with me,' he added drily.

She risked saying, 'What could happen to me when
I'm with you? Your aunt says you used to be known as
Not Safe in Taxis, but that was a long time ago.'

He didn't answer. When she flicked a quick glance at
him, his expression made her wish she had held her
tongue.

'Not that long ago.' His voice was unnervingly silky.
'And remarks like that can be taken as a challenge. Never

provoke reactions you might not be able to cope with, *chica.*'

Knowing that it *had* been a challenge and mortified by his immediate recognition of an impulse she barely understood herself, she jumped up.

'I've had enough of being lectured.'

His reaction was frighteningly fast. She was scarcely on her feet before he was towering above her, his hand like a clamp on her shoulder.

'Sit down and drink your tea.'

'I don't want any.'

Attempting to break free, she ducked her shoulder and dodged. She might have known it wouldn't work. But this time it wasn't her arm he grabbed but the strap of her swimsuit and the strain of conflicting pressures was too much for the weakened threads attaching it to the fabric below her shoulder blade. The strap ripped free and, being held fast in his hand, caused the front of her suit to drag against the folds of the towel. Only loosely secured, it gave way. Before she could clutch it to her, she was topless, if only partially.

Raul let go of the strap. 'Sorry about that . . . but your swimsuit is past its best. How long have you had it?' He sounded amused.

Perhaps it was her confusion he found amusing. It was not as if what he had seen was anything special. At the beach resorts breasts were on show all the time, many of them far more spectacular than hers.

'We can't afford to replace things as often as most people,' she said, re-fixing the towel and trying not to blush. Then, in an attempt at composure, 'If you don't mind, I'll take my tea up to my room. Being damp is becoming uncomfortable.'

'Yes, I'd think you'd better,' he said. 'Good-night, Maria.'

*   *   *

Next day the drive from Uxmal to Mérida took them over the Puuc Hills from which could be seen the seemingly endless stretches of flatness on all sides.

By late morning they were in the first living city Maria had ever seen.

Speaking to Miss Dysart, who today had chosen to sit beside him, Diego said, 'In most Mexican towns, *señorita*, the main square is called the *zócalo*. But the Meridanos call this the *plaza grande*.'

Surrounded by historic buildings, the centre of the square was also a park where many people, mostly men, were sitting on benches in the shade of tall trees or taking shortcuts from one side of the square to the other by way of four wide intersecting walks.

'Do you see the white S-shaped seats... there at the side of each of the main paths?' Diego took a hand off the wheel to point them out. 'Those are love-seats called *confidenciales*. In the days when girls were chaperoned, they were permitted to sit on those seats to talk to their young men. Today tourists pose for photographs on them.'

From the square they drove along a busy main road, crowded with shoppers, until they came to a much grander thoroughfare bordered by wide tree-lined pavements and outdoor cafés.

'This is the Paseo de Montejo, built at the end of the last century in the style of the Champs Elysées in Paris,' said Diego. 'Here the wealthy plantation owners erected their mansions, importing Carrara marble and European antiques to furnish them. On your left is the Palacio Cantón, built for a general in 1909. Now it's a museum. Unfortunately some of the mansions have been demolished because it is now too expensive to use them as private houses. But one of the finest has been preserved as a hotel and that is where you are staying.'

Moments later he turned the car into the driveway of an immense white building with tall windows surrounded by stucco garlands and opening on to graceful balconies shaded by green awnings. The edge of the roof was adorned with stone urns and more urns planted with bright flowers flanked the steps leading up to the imposing entrance.

Raul had already arrived, having flown himself to Mérida in a fraction of the time it had taken them to arrive. He was waiting for them by the fountain in the hotel's palatial hall. With him was Mr Huntingdon who had also reserved a room here, setting out from Uxmal an hour before them.

A member of the managerial staff conducted them upstairs to a suite of rooms on the first floor. The hub of the suite was a drawing-room with French windows overlooking an awning-shaded terrace and garden leading to another terrace round a large swimming pool.

'What a contrast to our mole-like quarters in other places,' said Miss Dysart, surveying the lofty ceiling and wide open spaces of her large double bedroom, while Maria was unpacking for her.

She herself had a single room, but even this was spacious and had its own marble bathroom and an ornate stained glass window.

They had lunch on the terrace downstairs, joined by Mr Huntingdon who, like Miss Dysart, always spent the early part of the afternoon resting.

'Are you going to swim, Raul?' his aunt asked, as the lift took them back to the suite.

He shook his head. 'I've some calls to make and a long fax from London I need to study and answer. I may swim later. Which reminds me . . . I have something for you, Maria.'

While his aunt disappeared for her rest and Maria waited in the sitting-room, he went into his room, leaving the door wide open so that she could see the wide double bed he was going to sleep in tonight.

He came back with a small soft package wrapped in fancy paper and adorned with an ornamental bow. 'I saw it in one of the showcases in the dining-room corridor but it comes from a shop in town so if you don't like it, or it doesn't fit you, it can be changed.'

Wondering what it could contain, she unfastened the parcel, trying to remove the bits of transparent sticky tape without tearing the silver and gold striped paper. Inside, swathed in tissue, were some small pieces of sky-blue silky stuff. At first she didn't realise what they were.

'It's a replacement for your black swimsuit,' said Raul.

'Oh...' She realised that she was holding a halter top and a tiny pair of briefs. 'It's very kind of you. Thank you. But you needn't have bothered. I've mended the strap of my black one.'

'It didn't flatter you,' he said. 'You'll look much nicer in this. But, as I say, if it's the wrong size, we'll go to the shop later on and change it for another.' He paused, before adding, 'If it does fit, don't be shy about wearing it. You have a very nice figure.'

He went into his room and closed the door.

Maria was reading when Miss Dysart emerged from her bedroom with some clothes to be pressed.

'And when you've organised that, we'll have tea before going shopping. Mr Huntingdon has the address of the best place to buy Panama hats.'

To Maria's surprise, Raul accompanied them on the hat-buying expedition. As they set out, walking four abreast on the Paseo's expanse of pavement, he said,

'You haven't brought the swimsuit so I conclude it was OK.'

'Yes, thank you. It's fine. But you must let me pay you for it. I can't let you buy it for me.'

'Why not? It's the least I can do, after ripping your old one.'

To her disappointment he fell back a pace in order to change places and walk alongside Mr Huntingdon.

The following afternoon, while her employer was resting and Raul was busy writing reports for whoever employed him, Maria went to look for the house where her mother had grown up.

It wasn't difficult to find but clearly it was a long time since anyone had lived there.

She was peering through the railings when she had the feeling someone was watching her. Turning round, she saw a small, plump woman eyeing her from the opposite pavement.

Maria smiled at her. '*Buenas tardes, señora.*'

'*Buenas tardes.*'

'I was admiring this house,' said Maria, in Spanish. 'Do you know how long it's been empty?'

'Fifteen years.' The woman came across the road. 'It was a fine house. I worked there. I took you for a tourist,' she added. 'It's your hair that makes you look like a foreign visitor. Can that colour be natural?'

Maria nodded. 'Yes, but I am a visitor here, although I was born not far away. So you knew the house when it was occupied, *señora*?'

'No one better. I worked for the owners for twenty-three years. For the first few years after they left, when they hoped to sell it, I kept it swept and aired. But it won't sell now. Big old houses aren't wanted any more. The only people who take an interest these days are art-

ists and photographers. I've had several asking me to let
them into the garden. Would you like to have a look
round?'

'If you can spare the time.'

'I've plenty of time since my husband died and my
children left home. Come.' The woman took a bunch of
keys from her pocket and unlocked the padlock fastening
the rusty chain securing the tall wrought iron gates.

They creaked as she pushed one open and ushered
Maria into the forsaken garden. 'Watch out for scor-
pions,' she warned. 'Mostly they stay hidden under the
plant pots but sometimes I see the little devils scuttling
about.'

'Why did the owners leave?' Maria asked.

'They had a lot of bad luck. They weren't young when
I started work here. Doña Julia was about forty and her
husband, Don Jaime, about ten years older. They already
had three sons who were nearly grown-up and then, as
so often happens, she became pregnant again. But they
had plenty of money, so it wasn't a worry to them. How
they loved that child!'

'What did they call her?' asked Maria, although she
had little doubt that it was her mother they were talking
about.

'Isela ... the prettiest child you ever saw. But very
spoilt, not only by her parents but by her brothers. They
all adored her. So she grew up accustomed to having her
own way in everything ... until she was about your age.'

'What happened then?'

'The same thing that happens to all young girls. She
fell in love. Then, for the first time, her father put his
foot down.'

'Why?'

'He'd already picked out a husband for her. A friend
of her eldest brother ... suitable in every way. The man

she wanted was impossible...an American...no money or prospects and much too old for her. But you can't spoil a girl all her life and expect her to toe the line when she's head over heels in love. Isela was as headstrong as they come. She ran off to Guatemala with her *gringo*. She wrote to tell them not to worry about her—her mother was frantic, poor soul—and the next thing they heard, she was pregnant. So that was the end of that!'

'What do you mean?' asked Maria, although she already knew the answer.

'Don Jaime was terribly angry. He was already in bad health and his anger brought on a stroke which left him a permanent invalid. It broke Doña Julia's heart but she gave orders that Isela's name was never to be spoken in his presence. But I know that her daughter wrote to her and I think the *señora* replied. Anyway less than a year later they heard that Isela had died giving birth to a child.' The caretaker's lugubrious tone was tinged with a certain relish in relating this catalogue of disasters.

'How did they find that out?'

'I suppose the father must have written to them. But he wouldn't give the child up. Doña Julia sent her eldest son to reason with him, but it was no use. They were preparing to take him to court when Doña Julia herself died. The strain of nursing her husband and worrying about Isela and the baby was too much for her. She was hardly in her grave when Don Jaime had another stroke and became completely bedridden. So his son became head of the family and he decided to build a more modern house, which would be easier to run.'

'What a sad story,' said Maria. 'But Isela's three brothers... have they done well in life?'

'Very well indeed. They're men in their fifties now, as important and respected as their father was in his time. They all live in fine houses in the new smart part of town and I saw a photograph of the youngest of Don Jaime's granddaughters in *Por Esto*! a few days ago. The picture was taken at the party for her twenty-first birthday. Such a lovely girl. She'll be married before long.'

Maria wondered what the caretaker would say if she told her that in fact it was she, Maria, who was the youngest of the late Don Jaime's granddaughters.

'You say the sons live in the new smart part of town. Could you give me an address? A friend of mine is a foreign journalist. I think he might like to ask their permission to take photographs of this house as an example of the architecture of times gone by,' she said.

'He would have to speak to the eldest son, Don Guillermo. If you have a pen in your bag, you had better write the address down or you may forget it.'

Although the woman was obviously lonely and glad of someone to talk to, Maria sensed she was also hoping for a *propina*. The dress she was wearing was a traditional *huipil* but instead of the yoke being embroidered it was cut from a piece of floral cotton. This might be an economy or it might be that, with the advent of television, city women no longer plied their needles as diligently as in the past. Before they parted, she gave the caretaker a modest tip.

A few blocks on she asked another woman to direct her to the address she had written down. It took her about half an hour to get there and there wasn't much to be seen. Her uncle lived in a large single-storey house surrounded by a high wall. Only the roof and the upper branches of several jacarandas, the doors of a garage large enough to house several cars, were visible from the street. The sole resemblance between this house and the delapidated mansion where her grandparents had lived was a handsome pair of wrought-iron gates. If she went up close and peered through she might get a glimpse of the entrance to the house. But if she did that someone inside might see her and find her interest suspicious.

For a while she lingered under a tree on the far pavement, wondering how she would be received if she rang the bell and introduced herself as Don Guillermo's long-lost niece. Would they be pleased to see her? Or, because of the distress her mother's elopement had caused all those years ago, would they identify her with the man who had lured Isela away and want nothing to do with his daughter?

Even if they welcomed her, she knew her father would consider it a betrayal of his trust in her. Much as she longed to meet them, she knew she could never make contact without her father's consent, which he would never give.

Hot, tired and depressed by the unbridgeable gulf separating her from the numerous cousins with whom, in other circumstances, she might have grown up and been close friends, she walked slowly back in the direction of the hotel.

In the Paseo de Montejo she stopped at an ice-cream parlour and spent the last half-hour of her free time slowly eating a refreshing lime ice and thinking about Isela, the rebellious girl who had been her mother and whose defiance of her parents' wishes had had such a tragic conclusion, not only for herself but for them.

'Hello, Maria. May I join you?'

She came out of her reverie to find Raul standing beside her.

'Of course... but it's nearly time for me to go back.'

He glanced at his watch. 'There's no hurry. Would you like another ice?'

'No, thank you.'

'Then have a cold drink. Although——' with an appraising glance '—you never look hot and sticky like most tourists, if you've spent the afternoon exploring you'll need to top up your fluid level.' He ordered an ice for himself and *agua de limón* for her before asking, 'Where did you go?'

'Nowhere in particular. I just wandered around looking at houses. This isn't at all the way I imagined a big city.'

'Mérida isn't like most cities. It has eight hundred thousand inhabitants but it feels like a large market town and doesn't have the street crime you'd expect in a place this size. I wouldn't have let you go out on your own in Mexico City.'

Before she could answer there was an outburst of hooting followed by a screech of tyres as a passing car did an emergency stop a short distance past the ice-cream parlour and then backed up until it was level with them.

The driver was a girl with a mass of dark curly hair who jumped out of the car and came dashing towards Raul, her pretty face alight with pleasure.

'Raul! What are you doing here? Why didn't you let us know you were in town, you bad man? How divine to see you.' She gave him both hands and tilted her face for his kiss.

Watching them exchange the cheek-kisses of people who were either related or close friends, Maria took her to be in her early twenties and, judging by the expensive sports car and the quality of her clothes and jewellery, either the daughter or wife of a very rich man.

However when Raul introduced her as Carolina González Perez, Maria saw that, although she wore several rings, her wedding finger was bare.

'My grandfather's sister, Iris Dysart, is over here on a visit and Maria has kindly volunteered to interpret for her when I'm not around,' he explained.

'Why didn't you warn us you were coming? You must come to the party tonight. We're celebrating César's engagement. My grandparents will enjoy talking to your old aunt, and I want to hear what you have been doing since I last saw you.'

'I shall have to consult Aunt Iris... and your mother may not wish to have three extra guests foisted on her,' said Raul.

'She won't mind. We're having a hundred people. What difference will three more make?' Carolina said, shrugging.

'You're going to get a parking ticket if you leave your car there much longer,' said Raul.

'Not at this time of day. But yes, I must go. I'm already late for my hair appointment. See you later.' With a flirtatious smile for him and a waggle of the fingers for Maria, she ran back to the car and was soon shooting away from the kerbside with a farewell tattoo on her horn.

Raul watched her departure with an amused shake of the head. 'That girl is a human hurricane,' he said, as he sat down. 'She ought to have been allowed to channel her energy into a career, but her parents have old-fashioned ideas about the best career for a woman. As none of the eligible young men they've lined up for her has passed muster, she amuses herself running a dress shop. Although most of the hard work is done by her assistant while Carolina skips off to New York, London and Paris to look for stock and enjoy herself,' he added drily.

'Have you known her long?'

'All my life. Her great-grandfather and my great-grandmother were brother and sister. Carolina's forebears were *hacendados* whose sisal plantations made them so much money that her grandparents were able to send their son to English public schools and their daughters to French finishing schools. In those days the peninsula was difficult to reach from Mexico City. So the wealthy Yucatán families had more contact with Europe than with their own centres of culture. Carolina's great-great-aunt married one of her brothers' English schoolfriends...my great-grandfather Richard Dysart.'

It occurred to Maria that Carolina's family and her own maternal relations must have moved in the same circles and perhaps still did. It might be that her uncles and aunts by marriage would be among the guests at the party tonight. After so long an interval, would they remember the surname of the man her mother had run off with? And if they didn't, would they recognise her? Her father had often told her that she had her mother's eyes and mouth.

If she met them by accident, as it were, and they did discern the likeness, would they acknowledge her? How could her father be angry with her if the contact with her mother's family came about by chance rather than by an initiative on her part?

'You seem a little *distraite* this afternoon, Maria,' said Raul. 'Something on your mind?'

'Not really. It's very hot here. I'm not used to walking on pavements.'

'Or to breathing traffic fumes,' he said, as several cars roared past.

The afternoon lull was ending and the wide boulevard, built for the horse-drawn *calesas* of which only a few remained, would soon be streaming with cars returning to the city after the siesta.

When she attempted to pay for her ice-cream, he smiled and said, 'No way. This is Mérida, where it's still a male prerogative to pick up the bill and both sexes like it that way. In America and Europe the rules have changed. A lot of women get their hackles up at the slightest hint of what they perceive as male condescension, even when it's not intended as such. Here, chivalry still rules.'

As they crossed the road, with his fingers holding her lightly above the elbow, he said, 'I hope, when you fly the nest, as you'll have to sooner or later, you won't let yourself be brainwashed into thinking of men as a hostile species.'

'Why should I do that?'

'The feminist extremists are a powerful lobby. And the fact that you've spent your life dominated by a man who—as all creative artists must—gives his work priority over everything makes you particularly susceptible to that lobby's propaganda.'

As they entered the hotel, Miss Dysart was emerging from the lift. They went through the building to the garden to sit with her while she had tea.

When she heard about the party, she said, 'How nice. But shall I be able to talk to anyone?'

'Oh, yes, no problem,' Raul assured her. 'At least half the people there will speak English or French.'

'Will the clothes we have with us be sufficiently formal?'

'Certainly. Just dress as you do for dinner and Maria can wear the *huipil* she wore at Cobá. Most of the men may be in tuxedos but I shall get by with a long-sleeved *guayabera*.'

'Excuse me, *señor*, there's a gentleman at the desk asking for Mees Dysart,' said one of the desk staff. 'He gave his name as Eriksen.'

'Send him through,' said Raul. Turning to his aunt, he translated what had been said.

'How clever of him to find us. I hoped we'd see him again.'

A few moments later Chris appeared, bearing a large bunch of flowers.

'For me? My dear boy, how kind of you,' she said, when he presented them to her.

'On the contrary, they're an inadequate token of my gratitude for your kindness to me,' he said formally.

'Maria, would you take these upstairs and ask the housekeeper for a vase, please? Just put them in water. I'll arrange them later.' Miss Dysart handed over the flowers and her room key. 'You are just in time to take tea with us, Christian, or perhaps you'd prefer a cold drink. Raul, would you catch the waiter's eye?'

It took Maria some time to procure a suitable container and leave the flowers soaking in it on Miss Dysart's bathroom counter. As she left the bedroom, Raul was coming out of his room on the opposite side of the corridor. He was wearing the cotton robe supplied by the hotel and had a pool towel slung over his shoulder.

'I'm going to cool off in the pool and I'm sure Aunt Iris will leave you *à deux* before long. She is far too shrewd not to realise that presenting her with a bouquet wasn't your friend's main motive in coming here,' he said quizzically. 'You don't have to come with us tonight, you know. If he wants you to go out with him, feel free.'

Was it a diplomatic hint that he would prefer not to take her with them to a family gathering?

'But there'll be a lot of young people there who might be useful contacts for you,' he went on. 'You can go out with Eriksen another night. It's up to you.'

'I expect Chris has made some new friends where he's staying. He only came by as a courtesy to your aunt,' she said, as the lift opened.

'I doubt that,' he said drily. 'He wouldn't have bothered if you hadn't been with her.'

'Perhaps he has better manners than you had at his age,' she said lightly.

Rather to her surprise, this rejoinder seemed to annoy him. They were standing facing each other and suddenly the teasing gleam had gone and his eyes were cold. 'You may be right.'

On impulse she said, 'I'm sorry...I didn't mean to sound rude.'

As she spoke the lift stopped, the door slid back and a couple stepped in, saying, *'Buenas tardes.'*

Both Raul and Maria murmured the polite response. Moments later they reached the ground floor where the woman stepped out first and the man waited for Maria to precede him.

Raul came out last, his expression still stern and withdrawn. He made no reference to her apology.

As they walked back to the garden, she felt his displeasure like a cloud across the sun. It was then that she realised she had fallen in love with him.

CHAPTER SIX

IN THE garden, Miss Dysart and Chris had been joined by Conrad Huntingdon just back from an expedition to see the flamingoes at Laguna Rosada.

When he had finished telling them about it, Raul excused himself to go to the pool and Miss Dysart said, 'You look as if you've had enough sun for one day, Mr Huntingdon. You and I are not as accustomed to it as these two.' She turned to the two young people. 'You won't mind if we leave you to bask while we withdraw to the shade of the terrace, will you?'

'Have you found somewhere nice to stay?' Maria asked, when their elders had gone off together.

'I met a Swedish couple at the market who told me about a guest house in Calle 68. It doesn't look much from the outside but you'd like the interior. The kitchen is painted like Frida Kahlo's. You know who I mean?'

She nodded. 'Diego Rivera's wife. Father has a book about her. Who else is staying there?'

'Mostly Americans. There are only seven rooms. I was lucky to get in. Tonight I'm going to have supper at Los Almendros. Can you come with me?'

'I'm sorry, Chris, I can't. We've been asked to a party. Raul has relations in Mérida.'

As the party didn't start until ten, they had a light supper in the hotel dining-room beforehand. Mr Huntingdon ate with them. Apparently he was also coming to the party. Maria concluded that Miss Dysart had asked Raul to ask their hosts if they might bring a fourth. Which

118

suggested she had taken a great liking to him...perhaps more than a liking.

Did people fall in love at Miss Dysart's age? Maria wondered. If they did, it must be a different, calmer form of love than this disturbing condition she found herself in.

What with wondering if Raul was still put out, and whether anyone would recognise her as Isela's daughter, she found it difficult to concentrate on the conversation at the table.

'You don't seem to have your usual good appetite this evening,' said Miss Dysart, noticing that Maria had put her knife and fork together with some food left on her plate.

'I'm sorry...I'm not very hungry.'

'Just as well to leave a corner for whatever we may be offered later,' said Mr Huntingdon. He turned to Raul. 'It's extremely kind of your relations to allow me to join you. I hope my Spanish isn't too rusty for me to make intelligent conversation.'

Maria was grateful to him for distracting attention from her. While he was speaking a waiter whisked her unfinished *chiles en nogada* away.

In spite of her mingled excitement and apprehension, she managed to eat the dessert with an appearance of enjoyment and hoped that the partly wasted main course had been forgotten by the time they left the table.

But as they were leaving the dining-room, Raul bent towards her and said in a low tone, 'Is your tummy all right?'

'Yes, perfectly, thank you.'

'I wouldn't expect Montezuma to single you out, but one can never be certain. He revenges himself on the just and the unjust equally.' He smiled at her. 'You look charming. I like the hairstyle and you haven't overdone the make-up this time.'

The compliment made her glow. 'Thank you.'

Diego had been given the evening off and Raul was their driver tonight.

'Come in front with me, Maria,' he said, when the car was brought round from a garage somewhere at the rear by one of the hotel staff.

That she was no longer in his black books boosted her courage for the evening ahead; perhaps a momentous one.

Although the most crucial day of her life, now and always, had to be the morning she had gone to Playa and met Raul.

The house to which they were bidden was ablaze with lights, its drive already filled with cars which also lined the street outside and several nearby streets.

'I can't very well drop you off as you don't know your host and hostess, Aunt Iris,' said Raul. 'I'm afraid you'll have to walk a little way.'

'We don't mind that, do we, Mr Huntingdon? We are not *quite* on our last legs.'

'Happily no,' he agreed. 'I hope to be gadding about for some time yet, and you obviously feel the same way. Where are you planning to go next?'

While they were discussing possible destinations, Raul glanced at Maria and winked. That the suggestion of a smile and the flicker of an eyelid should give her so much pleasure was absurd, but it was so. She wondered if he also thought his great-aunt might be susceptible to the gallantries of the still debonair Englishman.

A number of people in evening dress were converging on the house as they strolled along the tree-shadowed streets of what was clearly a rich and exclusive neighbourhood.

Evidently Carolina had been looking out for them. They had scarcely entered the driveway before she was hurrying to meet them, looking very attractive with her hair up and wearing long diamanté earrings which glittered in the light of the garden's expensive illuminations. She was wearing a white satin camisole with a short black silk skirt edged with satin and black satin shoes.

As she and Raul repeated the kisses they had exchanged earlier, and he introduced her to Miss Dysart, Maria had a sinking feeling she might be the only person present with bare legs and wearing a *huipil*. Carolina's pretty legs were veiled by sheer black tights, or perhaps they were a pair of the lace-topped stockings Maria had seen in one of the magazines Raul had brought to her room at Cobá.

'*Mucho gusto, señorita.*' Mr Huntingdon bowed over her hand.

Then Maria said good evening and saw the older girl's eyes take in her home-made dress and the hairstyle she had done herself.

Turning away, Carolina said, in English, 'Come and meet my parents, Mees Dysart.'

When she saw their host and hostess receiving their guests at the entrance to a large luxurious room filled with smart people drinking champagne and beyond it, a glimpse of more people standing about on a lantern-lit terrace, Maria felt momentarily terrified.

Her mother had grown up in this milieu and had belonged here. But she didn't. Suppose no one spoke to her? Could she bear the mortification of standing about by herself, ignored apart from some puzzled glances as people wondered what an obvious outsider was doing here?

Then, as Carolina was asked by her mother to look after Miss Dysart and her escort until she had finished receiving, and they disappeared into the throng, a hand fell lightly on Maria's shoulder and, as a waiter came by with a tray of glasses, Raul took one and put it into her hand.

'Come and have a look round the garden with me,' he said, taking a glass for himself.

And because he was with her, head and shoulders taller than most of the other men present, people drew aside to let them through and looked at them both with curiosity and interest.

The room smelt of women's scent, men's cologne, cigars and cigarettes, and the lavish arrangements of flowers reflected in ornate gilt mirrors. Maria found the combination cloying and was glad when they reached the fresher air of the terrace.

Beyond it, on a lower level, was a large swimming pool lit by underwater spotlights which made the still surface gleam like the huge square-cut blue-green gem she had noticed on a woman's hand as they came through the main reception-room.

'I expect you find all this a bit daunting, don't you?' said Raul, his hand sliding from her shoulder to the small of her back as he steered her in the direction of the steps to the lower level.

'I do rather,' she admitted. 'Especially as I seem to be the only person here in a *huipil*.'

'No, you aren't. There are several women here in *huipiles*. And you have the distinction of being the only natural blonde. Fair hair very rarely looks right with brown eyes, but in your case it does. You're going to receive a great many compliments. Don't let them go to your head,' he said, looking down at her with an expression not dissimilar from the one she remembered from the veranda of the old hacienda at Chichén Itza.

Whereupon a very good-looking young man in a white suit disengaged himself from a group of young people and came over to them.

'Raul... this is a nice surprise. Carolina told me you were in town, but she said you were bringing two people of the old generation, not someone of mine,' he said, smiling at Maria.

'Juanito is Carolina's youngest brother,' Raul told her. To Juanito, he added, 'This is Maria's first big party. She knows no one, except for briefly meeting your sister, and she's a little shy. Can I rely on you to take care of her while I pay my respects to your elders?'

'But of course, it will be my pleasure,' said Juanito. 'But first we'll get to know each other a little. Shall we sit over there, Maria?' indicating a cushioned bench in an alcove.

An hour later she wondered why she had felt she might be cold-shouldered. Apart from a couple of girls who were polite but not very forthcoming, everyone else was friendliness itself.

When her first glass was empty and another waiter had come round with a selection of drinks, she had taken a glass of papaya juice. She was glad she had tried the champagne, and perhaps it had helped her to overcome her initial nervousness, although that was mainly Juanito's doing. But she hadn't much liked the taste of the sparkling wine. Ice-cold fruit juice was far more refreshing.

While they were in the line up for the buffet, she asked Juanito if his parents knew her mother's eldest brother, although she referred to her uncle only by name and didn't mention her relationship to him.

'Of course. Papa does business with him. But he and his wife are abroad now. Why do you ask?'

She explained about seeing the old house and being told by the caretaker who owned it.

'It's just as well he isn't here,' said Juanito. 'If you'd mentioned that rundown old place, you'd have put your foot in it.'

'Why?'

'Oh, it has to do with something that happened years ago ... something they still don't talk about. You know how stuffy and conventional people of that age are. Mamá knows the story. She told Carolina about it as a warning of what can happen to girls who don't pay attention to what their parents tell them. I forget all the details.' He lowered his voice, so that the people in front and behind wouldn't overhear. 'Don Guillermo had a sister who ran off and got herself pregnant. But she died having the baby, so it wasn't too difficult to hush it up.'

'Did your mother know his sister?'

'I expect so. In Mérida everybody knows everybody. You can't put a foot out of line without the whole town hearing about it. That's why Carolina likes going to New York and Paris. She can get up to anything she likes there.'

Later, after supper, the tinkling of a bell drew everyone's attention to the fact that his father was going to make a speech from the terrace about his eldest son's betrothal. The people in the house crowded into the garden to hear him and Maria saw Carolina coming out with Raul close behind her. When she perched herself on the stone balustrade he took up a position behind her, gripping the outer edge of the capping stones so that his outstretched arm would prevent her from over-balancing into the garden.

While the engaged couple and both sets of parents were taking up their positions, Carolina leaned back against Raul, tilting her head to speak to him. Perhaps she was keeping her voice low to say something confidential. He bent his head forward to hear. To Maria, watching them, their postures expressed a degree of intimacy which was curiously painful to see. Had they met each other away from Mérida, in the places where the Mexican girl was able to shrug off the stricter conventions of her home town? Had they been lovers?

A hush fell over the garden as Juanito's father began to speak of the pleasure it gave him and his wife to announce the forthcoming marriage of their son César to Ana-Luisa, a girl with all the best qualities of her sex.

As he began to enumerate these—modesty, a sweet disposition, devotion to her parents—it occurred to Maria that perhaps she ought to be with Miss Dysart, translating. But then she remembered that Mr Huntingdon spoke some Spanish so probably he was interpreting the speech, or would do so afterwards.

After a similar speech by Ana-Luisa's father in praise of his prospective son-in-law and in-laws, the guests were invited to revisit the dining-room where the second phase of the buffet was now awaiting their pleasure.

'Come: we'll slip in the back way so that you can see the *postres* while they look their best,' murmured Juanito, taking Maria by the hand and leading her through a shrubbery to a side door.

A few minutes later her eyes widened in astonishment at the spectacle of the flower-garlanded tables now set out with spectacular arrangements of tropical fruits, billowing confections of meringue and spun sugar, and silver platters of ice-creams decorated with the fruit and nuts with which they were flavoured. She had read of such puddings in books but had never expected to taste them.

'Did your mother make all these?' she exclaimed.

Juanito laughed. 'Mamá hasn't done any cooking since I was in short trousers and Carolina can't boil rice. It's all been done by caterers.'

'Trust you to be one of the first here, greedy one,' said a voice. They turned to face his mother. 'Juanito is like me . . . he loves sweet things,' she said indulgently to Maria. 'Is he looking after you properly?'

'Perfectly, thank you, *señora.*'

'I must compliment you on your dress, my dear. Several people have commented on it. The design is most unusual . . . and such exquisite needlework. It's nice to see a girl of your age choosing the traditional style in preference to modern fashions. Did you buy it from a store or was it made privately for you?'

'I made it myself, *señora.*'

'You did? But that's remarkable. My daughter has a problem threading a needle. I don't know of any girls who sew beautifully now. Raul tells me you live on the east coast and have never been to Mérida, and yet I feel your face is familiar . . . that I've seen you somewhere before. Where can we have met?'

'I'm sure we haven't, *señora* . . . which is why it's particularly kind of you to allow me to come to this wonderful celebration.'

'Anyone who is a friend of Raul's is always welcome in this house. Excuse me . . . there are so many people I must have a word with.' She lingered a moment longer, her eyes on Maria's face and a puzzled frown contracting her fine black eyebrows. 'There's something about you . . . but I can't quite place what it is.' With a slight shrug of plump shoulders, she smiled and turned away.

* * *

The festivities were still in full swing when at one o'clock in the morning Raul's party took their leave.

'I fear we are dragging you away,' said his great-aunt as they left the house.

'Not at all. I burnt my candle at both ends at César's age, but I'm no longer a night owl. If you'll wait here, I'll bring the car round.' He left them, moving down the road at a long-legged lope. As everyone living round-about had been invited to the house they were leaving, neither his footsteps nor the murmur of their voices was going to disturb any sleepers.

'Such energy at this time of night!' said Miss Dysart. 'I suppose you are still wide awake too, Maria? Did you enjoy yourself?'

'Very much. I've never seen such lovely clothes . . . or such food.'

'These people live well, don't they?' said Mr Huntingdon. 'I was surprised by such a display of opulence after the extreme poverty I've seen driving through the villages in the centre of the province. Some Mexicans are existing in conditions as primitive as the life of most Africans. Others, such as these people, enjoy almost the same opulent lifestyle as the sisal millionaires in the past.'

They were still discussing the gulf between rich and poor when Raul came back with the car.

En route to the hotel, while the two behind them were still on the subject of Mexico's economy, he said to Maria, 'Carolina's mother says you remind her of someone. Do you know where your Mexican forebears lived? Could they have come from Mérida?'

She didn't want to lie to him, but neither did she want to tell him the truth.

'I don't know much about them. My father never talks about the past.'

'Do you have a picture of your mother?'

'Only a portrait he painted which doesn't show her full face.'

'So you don't know how much you're like her?'

'I believe I'm more like Father's Norwegian great-grandmother.'

'A lot of people noticed you tonight and were intrigued by the combination of your Mexican eyes and your dress and that Nordic hair. Did Juanito try to make a date?'

'He suggested taking me out tomorrow but I explained why I was here.'

Miss Dysart must have overheard this part of the conversation. She leaned forward and said, 'If Juanito wants to take you out, by all means go with him. I'm going bird-watching in Conrad's car tomorrow, so you will have the day off, Maria.'

'In that case I'll avail myself of Maria's services,' said Raul. 'There's no point in encouraging Juanito to lose his notoriously susceptible heart to her. He's supposed to be keeping his mind on his studies right now. He's a bright lad, but chronically lazy. His father wasn't best pleased with me for introducing him to another potential distraction. He was relieved to hear Maria wouldn't be around long.'

'Well, as long as our outing doesn't leave her at a loose end,' said Miss Dysart.

'It won't do that,' replied Raul, and he gave Maria a sideways glance which made her heart skip a beat.

But later, when she was in her room and undressing, the exciting prospect of spending a day alone with him was modified by the memory of Carolina sitting on the balustrade, leaning back against his chest in a manner suggesting that their bodies had often been in even closer contact.

In the bathroom, a luxury she still wasn't used to, she washed her face, carefully wiping her mouth with a tissue to make sure no trace of lipstick was left before she used one of the several towels.

She guessed that by the time Juanito's mother went to bed, she would be far too tired to lie awake pondering why Maria's face had struck a chord in her memory. But would the elusive likeness be still on her mind tomorrow? Would she go on trying to recall what it was about her unexpected guest which had seemed familiar?

Perhaps not. Perhaps her busy domestic and social life did not allow very much time for brain-searching.

But remembering was sometimes involuntary, thought Maria, as she climbed into bed. Forgotten scenes, places and people, would suddenly spring to mind apparently of their own accord.

It wasn't impossible that tomorrow one of the other guests would telephone to thank her hostess for the party. Miss Dysart disapproved of telephoning. She was going to convey her thanks by letter and had suggested that Maria should also write a note.

However, if one of their hostess's close friends rang up to discuss the party with her, and asked why a girl with blonde hair had been wearing a *huipil*, it might occur to Señora de González to visualise what Maria would look like with hair as dark as her daughter's. And then it might dawn on her why she seemed vaguely familiar.

CHAPTER SEVEN

NEXT morning, after they had waved goodbye to the bird-watchers, Raul said, 'Is there anything special you'd like to do today?'

'I'd like to go to the museum of crafts and costume, but I expect you've been there before and have more important things to do.'

'Is that a diplomatic way of saying that you'd rather spend the day with Eriksen?'

She shook her head. 'Chris has gone...he's on his way to Campeche. I just don't want you to feel you have to look after me.'

'I enjoy your company, Maria.'

Did he mean it? she wondered, as they set out. But why should he bother to accompany her if he didn't?

After looking round the museum, they spent the rest of the morning exploring some more of the city before returning to the hotel for lunch.

Carolina was waiting for them in the lobby. She favoured Maria with two perfunctory social kisses before greeting Raul.

'I thought you'd spend most of today catching up on sleep,' he said as he straightened.

'I'm used to going to bed at dawn,' she said airily. 'Mamá is exhausted, but before she went to bed she had an idea she asked me to tell you about. Why don't you take Tia Iris to our beach house on Cozumel for a few days? The Englishman as well, if you like.'

'That's very kind of your mother. I'll suggest it to them. Will you join us for lunch, Carolina?'

'I was hoping you'd ask me.' She gave him an intimate look. 'It was a shame you had to leave early last night. As for the beach house...it keeps the maids on their toes to have visitors to look after. With nothing to do, they get slack.'

The move from Mérida to the island was made by a local airline and, although the short flight was no big deal to the others, to Maria it was yet another magical experience, for it showed her the coast where she had grown up from a new perspective, and the colours and translucency of the sea were even more beautiful seen from the air.

It had come as no surprise to her when Carolina had decided to join them on Cozumel. Indeed Maria suspected that this was the real object of the exercise and that it was the Mexican girl, not her mother, who had conceived the beach house plan.

Her theory was confirmed when, on their first evening there, she heard Carolina saying to Miss Dysart, 'If Maria is homesick and wants to go back to her father, I'd be happy to interpret for you.'

To her relief, the old lady's reply was, 'Thank you, Carolina, but I should prefer to retain Maria's services until I leave Mexico.'

The house was built on a rocky promontory and at night the sea below the terrace where they dined was lit by powerful lamps attached to the *palapa* which made it possible to see the crowds of fish competing for the bread Carolina threw to them.

Had it not been for her presence, Maria would have had Raul to herself because it was increasingly clear that the two older people preferred each other's company.

One morning, at breakfast, Miss Dysart said she was thinking of prolonging her visit to Mexico and suggested that Maria should write to her father for permission to extend her leave of absence. But Maria felt she would have to ask him in person, and Raul agreed with her.

'Why don't we take the boat and sail over?' suggested Carolina. 'There's a strong breeze. It's perfect sailing weather.'

'By the time we get there and back, the wind may have stiffened. You're a good sailor. Maria may not be. Anyway the boat is too big for me to handle alone if a squall blows up.'

'We could pay one of the boys from the sail-and-dive shop at the hotel to come along. They all know how to crew,' Carolina suggested. 'The place is full of elderly Americans this week. The only people using the cats and the surfboards are the staff.'

'No, we'll go on the ferry,' Raul said firmly. 'That way I can check progress at the new resort while Maria is seeing her father.'

'In that case I'll stay here. The ferries are a bore. They smell of diesel——' Carolina wrinkled her nose '—and some of the people on them smell nasty too.'

'Fortunately Maria's sensibilities are less delicate than yours,' Raul replied. 'She'll enjoy the ferry.'

Carolina's eyes flashed. In the looks they exchanged Maria read signals she could not interpret.

Was the other girl saying, Of course? She's a guttersnipe. That's her milieu. But it isn't mine.

And had the message in Raul's eyes acknowledged the difference between them but warned her to make it less obvious?

Maria did enjoy the ferry. The passengers were a mixture of tourists and islanders and there was a strong whiff of fuel oil pervading the large saloon with its rows of high-backed seats divided by the central aisle. In the wider cross-aisle amidships a wheelchair, an openwork basket containing a dozen chicks and various bits of poor people's luggage had been put.

They sat in the seats on this aisle so that Raul had more room for his long legs. In front of them, screwed to the upper part of the bulkhead, was a colour television, one of several screens in the saloon. An American movie was being shown, with Spanish subtitles. She watched it, enthralled by the novelty, although later she was repelled by the realistic violence of a fight between two of the male characters. Flinching, she looked away and was disconcerted to find that Raul, whom she had thought intent on some papers he had brought with him, was watching her.

'I don't think you'd find TV very interesting if you saw it regularly,' he said. 'Life is too short to waste time being what's called a couch potato.'

'Don't you ever watch it?'

'Occasionally. I find reading and listening to music more relaxing. We're nearly there. I'll be occupied here for about an hour. Then I'll walk up the beach and say hello to your father myself. All right?'

In some ways she was glad to be back; padding along the firm sand at the water's edge, sometimes splashing through the shallows. But when the familiar *palapa* came in sight, her eagerness to see her father and pour out all her adventures was tinged with apprehension. Would he want to hear? Would he be pleased she was enjoying herself? Or would his attitude be disapproving and resentful? In the time she had been away, she had come to realise how abnormal their life together was, and how strange her father had become compared with a man like Conrad Huntingdon, whose view of his fellow men was tolerant and humorous.

Her father was lying in his hammock as she approached, but he didn't sit up and wave or come to meet her. She concluded he was asleep, although it was unusual for him to take a nap in the morning.

At the sight of a glass and a bottle of tequila on the sand underneath the hammock, she frowned. She had never known him to drink at this hour. Could they have been there since last night? Could he have drunk so much that he was still sleeping it off at eleven in the morning?

Another possibility occurred, making her heart miss a beat and her stomach clench with fear. She hurried nearer, terrified that a closer look might confirm that he wasn't sleeping but was dead. People did die at his age and he hadn't been looking well lately.

At first glance, George Rawlings' face made her smother a gasp of anguish. She knew he hadn't been as yellow as that when she'd left. Nor had his cheeks been as sunken as they were now.

But at that moment he stirred, shifting his position slightly.

'Father... are you all right?' Maria bent over him, touching him, her hands on his folded arms.

Startled and confused, he swore at her in Spanish before he recognised her.

'Oh... it's you. What are you doing here?'

'I came to see how you were. We're staying in Cozumel now. I came over on the ferry. I'll be home in a few days. Miss Dysart's visit is nearly over.'

Rawlings swung his bare feet to the ground on either side of the hammock and sat up, rubbing his eyes.

'A good thing too. I should never have let you go if I'd known why that crook was here.'

'What crook? What are you talking about?'

'Dysart of course. Who else? Since you left I've found out about him. D'you know who he is, the deceiving bastard? He's one of the big racketeers...one of the richest men in the resort business. He's already made millions in Europe, putting up cell-block hotels to cram with package tourists. Now he's doing it here. Raking in a fortune for himself and his shareholders. And to hell with the land and the people it really belongs to.'

'Father, I'm sure that's not true. Where did you hear such stories?'

For a moment he looked oddly furtive. Then he said gruffly, 'A few days after you left, I went to Cancún...thought it was time I had a check-up.'

Alarmed—he had always refused to have any truck with doctors—she said, 'What did they tell you?'

'Nothing I didn't know. I'm not a young man any more...can't expect to be as fit as I was.'

'But there's nothing specific wrong with you?'

'Only wear and tear...nothing they can put right. Anyway, while I was there I made some enquiries...found out who's putting up the money for that new resort complex. It's a company owned by Dysart. He's already as rich as Croesus and he's hell-bent on doubling his fortune. Men like that—greedy, powerful, unscrupulous—are the reason the world's in a mess. They don't give a damn for anyone but themselves.'

'Raul isn't like that. You don't know him.'

'And don't want to,' George Rawlings said brusquely. 'If I'd any idea who he was, I'd have spat in his eye the first time he came here.'

'He's coming to see you later on. Please don't be rude to him, Father. He's been very kind to me...so has his aunt. They're nice people, really they are. I'm sure if Raul is as rich as you say he is he does a lot of good with his money.'

'Oh, yes, I expect he plays the benefactor. Most of 'em do,' her father said cynically. 'But it's only a fraction of their real wealth that they dish out to selected charities. It's a form of self-promotion. It enhances their social status.'

Maria saw it was useless to argue with him. He had made up his mind and nothing would change his opinion.

'You haven't asked how I've been getting on,' she said quietly. 'Have you missed me?'

'It's been quiet without you, although I was glad to get back from Cancún. The noise there would drive you mad. I had to stay overnight to get the results of some tests and my room was over a disco. It was four o'clock in the morning before the row stopped.'

Half an hour later, out of the corner of her eye, Maria saw a distant figure striding along the beach. Long before he was clearly recognisable, she knew it was Raul by his height and the way he moved. In five or six minutes he would be with them. How would he react to being black-guarded by her father? Would he realise the older man had been drinking? That he was a sick man?

For although George Rawlings claimed the tests hadn't revealed anything specifically wrong, she was sure they had. The mere fact that he had gone to Cancún, a place he abominated, proved to her that he must have had some alarming symptoms. He looked ill. Even now, after going for a dip in the sea and shaving off several days' stubble and combing his hair, he still looked a bad colour and far more gaunt than when they had said goodbye.

There could be no question of her going back to Cozumel and leaving him. Not that he would allow her to go. He had already said so.

To Maria, watching Raul cross the last twenty yards of sand to where she and her father were waiting for him, was like seeing someone walk into an ambush and being unable to warn them.

For the rest of her life she would remember what it was like to be torn by conflicting loyalties. Beside her stood the man she had loved all her life, the *only* person she had loved. Approaching was the man she wanted to love and be loved by.

'Good morning, Mr Rawlings. How are you?'

Raul's greeting was for her father, but his smile included her.

'You're not welcome here, Dysart. You never would have been welcome if I'd known who you were.'

Raul's friendly expression faded. His darkly tanned face seemed to harden. But his tone was still pleasant as he said, 'I don't understand that remark.'

'Then let me explain it to you.'

For several minutes, her father expressed his views on exploitative property developers and the rape of the world's most beautiful coasts. She had heard him hold forth in this denunciatory vein before, but never with such vitriolic fluency.

She found herself wanting to shout at him to be quiet, that it wasn't fair to condemn a man without hearing what he had to say. But she stood quietly by, staring fixedly at the sea because she didn't dare to look at Raul's face and see him writing her father off as a madman and wishing he had never got involved with either of them.

At last her father drew breath, but only for a few seconds.

'If I haven't made myself clear, let me try to make it plainer,' he snapped. 'I want you out of here, Dysart, and I don't want you coming back. You can have my daughter's things left at the Hotel Molcas and we'll pick them up when it suits us. And you can keep her wages. She doesn't need your money. For a man your age to be as rich as they say you are, he has to have had his

fingers in some dirty deals. Neither Maria nor I wa
any part of your loot.'

'Perhaps your daughter would like to speak for herse
Mr Rawlings.' Raul looked at her. 'Well, Maria? Do yc
agree with your father?'

What did he expect her to say? That she didn't believ
a word of it. That her father was ill and more than
little crazy from a lifetime of loneliness, hardship an
the bitterness of failing to make his mark on the a
world.

'As my father has said, you're not welcome here, Rau
Please give my apologies to Miss Dysart. She doesn
need me now...if she ever did. But she was kind an
I'm grateful.'

He stared at her for a long moment, his grey eyes na
rowed against the bright light and unreadable.

'I see,' he said quietly. 'In that case I'll say *adios*!'

He turned and began walking back the way he ha
come.

'Good riddance!' With an angry snort, her father wer
through the crude shelter that was their house and di
appeared in the direction of the privy.

Maria remained where she was, watching Raul wal
out of her life, trying to fix in her memory the set c
his head, the straight spine, the broad shoulders an
narrow hips, the loose, easy stride which soon would l
lost to sight and never seen again.

More than anything in the world she wanted to ru
after him, to make him understand that she didn't b
lieve any of the accusations her father had flung at hin
But surely he must know that? And if he didn't, wha
was the use of trying to make him understand that h
first loyalty was to the man who had reared her an
cared for her?

'Oh, Raul...I love you,' she whispered aloud, feeling her heart and soul shrivel with the pain of being suddenly cut off from the happiness of being with him.

As the distance between them grew, her view of him blurred and shimmered. But although it was now close to noon and the hottest part of the day, the distortion was not caused by heat. She was seeing him through a haze of tears.

The next day, secretly, while her father was having his siesta, Maria wrote a letter to Miss Dysart.

She had taken a single sheet of notepaper and one matching envelope from a drawer in the writing table in the sitting-room at the hotel in Mérida. They were of thick, beautiful quality and she had meant to keep them as a memento of the luxury which had surrounded her there.

It pained her to have to give them up, but she had nothing else to write on unless she tore a page of lined paper from the cheap exercise book she had bought for her diary of the journey. She didn't want to write the letter on that, making Miss Dysart think she had so little education that she needed guidelines to keep her writing straight.

What would Raul have told the Englishwoman and Carolina? she wondered unhappily as she began.

Dear Miss Dysart,
I am very sorry my father's health has prevented me from coming back to Cozumel to say goodbye and to thank you for your many kindnesses to me. Visiting the Mayan cities and Mérida with you was an unforgettable experience. I am sincerely grateful for the opportunity. I hope you have a comfortable journey back to England.
Very sincerely and affectionately,
Maria

Reading it through, she wondered if 'affectionately' sounded presumptuous. But she couldn't cross it out so it would have to stand.

Having sealed the letter in the elegant pale grey envelope with the name of the hotel on the flap, she realised that her first intention—to ask one of Rosalba's family to post it to Cozumel for her—wasn't practicable. Very likely by the time it got there, Miss Dysart would have left.

Either she could have it taken to the Hotel Molcas and hope the desk clerk would remember to hand it over when her luggage was left with him, or she could send it care of Raul at the new resort complex. If he was as important and powerful as her father made out, anything with his name on it should be treated with respect.

It turned out that one of Rosalba's sons had been taken on as a labourer on the site of the complex. Rosalba said she would make sure he took it to the site office the following day.

Her errand accomplished, Maria returned to the beach to pace back and forth by the sea's edge, but always within call of the *palapa*. That her father had something serious the matter with him was no longer in question. He seemed to be wasting before her eyes. She suspected he was in pain and trying to deaden it with alcohol.

In the past George Rawlings had had long bursts of creative energy followed by periods of exhaustion. He claimed to be passing through one of those phases now. But Maria could find no evidence that he had been hard at work all the time she had been away. Nor did she think it was fatigue which made him spend so much time sleeping. Liquor was making him drowsy. He was using it as a palliative when he ought to be having proper treatment for whatever was wrong with him.

She wished he would tell her what it was. But she didn't dare ask for fear of provoking another outburst of rage. It might be that he needed an operation and hadn't the money to pay for it. She knew that medical treatment was very expensive and poor people often died from conditions which, in America, were curable.

Even there, so her father said, hospitals and medicines were prohibitively expensive without insurance. She was sure he had no insurance. Throughout history, artists had lived from hand to mouth, dependent on patronage. Had her father been a more amenable man, Raul might have become his patron. But her father would never compromise his principles. She admired him for it. At the same time her common sense told her that it couldn't be right to put principles before people as he had when he came between her mother and her family. A man devoted to his art should have thought twice before taking responsibility for a wife and child.

That evening he scarcely touched the meal she had prepared.

'I'm not hungry. Don't fuss. You're not dancing attendance on that old biddy now. I never did eat much when I was taking it easy. My appetite'll pick up in a few days...when I start working again.'

In the night, while he was asleep, Maria slipped out of her hammock and wandered down the beach where she sat with her arms round her knees, her bare toes kneading the still-warm sand.

She could see the lights of the island on the horizon and she wondered if Raul had already forgotten her existence and was flirting with Carolina. She was the sort of girl he would marry, when he married. They were two of a kind.

Maria herself was not anyone's kind. She was an outsider, a misfit. Even Chris Eriksen, although he was a
wanderer for the time being, had a normal family background and an orderly life to go back to.

Desperately lonely and anxious, she put her head on
her knees and found relief in tears.

The next morning her father seemed to have recovered
some energy. He decided he wanted to paint her.

As he set up his easel and posed her, Maria began to
wonder if she had allowed her imagination to run away
with her. Perhaps he had only seemed ill because, prior
to going away, she hadn't looked at him closely, hadn't
noticed him growing older. Perhaps it was merely the
contrast between his ageing appearance and Raul's
superb physique which had made him seem ill.

As the day passed, it was she rather than he who
flagged. Sitting still was harder than it looked and he
didn't allow her many rests. Intent on the portrait, he
seemed tireless. But she noticed, with revived disquiet,
that his energy was fuelled by frequent nips from another
bottle of tequila.

At lunchtime they swam together. As soon as her hair
was dry, he resumed work.

'Aren't you going to have a siesta?'

'Not today. I want to finish this.'

The afternoon seemed interminable but at last he gave
a satisfied grunt.

'It's done. You can rest now.'

She stretched her limbs like a cat, then stood up,
curious to see what she looked like seen through his eyes.

The portrait surprised her. He had always spoken dis-
paragingly of artists who flattered their sitters, elongating
and tightening necks, smoothing out wrinkles, giving a
sparkle to dull eyes. 'Warts and all' was George

Rawlings' motto. But he had flattered her. The girl in the painting was beautiful.

'Well ... do you like it?' he asked.

'Yes ... but it's not really me.'

'It will be...you wait and see.' He splashed some more tequila into the tumbler and drained it in a single gulp. 'I'm going to cool off.' He set off towards the sea.

She watched him go. He seemed to be lurching slightly. Her anxiety reanimated. Yesterday, in the absence of both her swimsuits, she had swum in a ragged old T-shirt and briefs. She began to unbutton the white shirt she had worn for the portrait.

By the time she had changed, her father was in the deeper water beyond the shallows. Not that the sea was really deep anywhere inside the reef and they never swam outside it. She had heard it said that between the island and the mainland there was a channel more than three thousand feet deep, where the current ran at five knots. Although she was a strong swimmer, the thought of swimming there frightened her.

As she walked down the beach to join him, she saw her father tread water for a few moments and then begin swimming at right angles to the shore. It surprised her that he should be feeling vigorous after a hard day's work with a lot of liquor but not much food inside him. He wouldn't keep that pace up long. Any moment now he would tire and rest for a few minutes, floating, before returning with a leisurely backstroke.

But he didn't. He kept on swimming. And suddenly, with a cold thrill of fear, she knew what was in his mind. He was heading for the reef and the dark blue ocean beyond it. He was not coming back ... ever.

She had always thought of panic as a state of frantic agitation. Now she discovered it wasn't. It was a form of paralysis. Her mind and body seemed locked, unable to think or act.

Out in the sunlit water, her father swam steadily on, his thin arms rising and falling with terrifying regularity, each stroke taking him further from the shore, nearer to the reef. Even if it were possible to overtake him, she couldn't make him turn back.

And then, from the direction of Playa, came the drone of a motor and she saw the white plume of a powerboat coming fast up the coast. Having no other means of signalling, she pulled off her T-shirt and began to wave it.

CHAPTER EIGHT

Darkness had fallen when someone in a neat green overall—not a nurse, they wore blue—brought her some food on a tray.

There was no one else in the waiting-room. Raul had disappeared and her father was still in the hands of the doctors.

Maria felt exhausted and slightly sick. She didn't want to eat, but she felt they might make a fuss if she didn't.

The chicken sandwiches, garnished with pieces of unfamiliar green things, were arranged on a fine china plate. The orange juice was in a small vacuum jug to keep it ice-cold. Even the tray was a pretty one. This wasn't a public hospital but a very expensive private clinic. Obviously Raul would settle the bill in the first instance and somehow she would have to pay him back. But she wasn't equal to coping with that problem now.

She still felt numbed by the shock of her father's averted suicide and the rapid succession of events after Raul and the Mexican had succeeded in bringing him ashore.

If she hadn't seen it for herself, she wouldn't have believed that in less than an hour after walking into the sea he would be in the hands of medical experts in Cancún. It was like a miracle. But she knew it was actually a demonstration of the power of immense wealth. The only miraculous aspect was that Raul had decided to come back at precisely that moment. Ten minutes later it might... *would* have been too late.

She had managed to eat two of the sandwiches and was sipping a second glass of orange juice when Raul came back. He was carrying a large shiny yellow container with white cord handles.

'Here are some clothes. You can change in the ladies' room across the corridor. Your father's still undergoing tests. They'll let us know the results as soon as they can.'

'Will they let me see him?'

'Of course, but at present he's under sedation.' He handed over the carrier. 'Go and put these on.'

She was still wearing the tattered T-shirt she had used as a flag and, in the panic-stricken urgency of the moment, had neglected to put on as the men in the boat saw her signal and swerved inshore.

Now, stripping it off in the washroom, and seeing in the mirror behind the handbasins the reflection of herself as Raul and his companion had seen her, she felt a faint twinge of embarrassment at having exposed her body as shamelessly as the women and girls on the tourist beaches.

Not that either of the men had shown any sign of noticing her naked torso. The instant they knew the reason for her signal, they had gone to the rescue, a rescue not accomplished easily, for her father had resisted. Without the help of the Mexican even Raul, strong as he was, might not have been able to subdue George Rawlings' last violent struggle to accomplish his intention.

He had seemed to have some kind of brainstorm followed by a collapse into semi-consciousness. She didn't think he had known he was being transferred from the boat to a stretcher and then, after a short drive in the ambulance belonging to the new resort, to the helicopter which had flown them to Cancún.

The dress box contained a blue denim skirt with a braided white leather belt threaded through the loops on the waistband, two short-sleeved striped cotton shirts, two white embroidered net bras, two pale blue cotton briefs, a pair of white espadrilles, a short white cotton nightdress and a zip-fastened bag of quilted, plasticised cotton containing a toothbrush and hairbrush and other toiletries.

Reared to conserve and recycle her possessions, she didn't put the T-shirt and her own briefs in the waste-bin under the counter, but folded them neatly and stuffed them into the plastic bag taken from the hairbrush before putting them in the carrier.

When she returned to the waiting-room, Raul was flicking through the pages of a magazine. He stood up, cast it aside and looked her over.

'That's better,' he said approvingly. 'I've eaten one of your sandwiches.'

'Have the others. I'm not hungry.'

'I don't suppose you are, poor kid. It takes time to recover from this sort of shock. We'll have a proper meal later. I've arranged for you to spend the night in a hotel very near here.'

He glanced at his watch. 'Aunt Iris and Conrad will be halfway to London by now. They flew direct from Cozumel to the airport here, and then on to Miami. I was going to fly here with them, but then something cropped up at the new complex and I crossed by the ferry, bringing your things with me. When they gave me your note to Aunt Iris, I decided to come and see if you were all right. Your father looked pretty groggy the day he sent me packing. I was worried about you...and with reason.'

At this point a doctor appeared, a woman in her mid-thirties wearing the V-necked white cotton tunic and trousers of all the medical staff. An identification tag was attached to the tunic pocket in which was a folded stethoscope.

After introducing herself, she suggested they should sit down.

'I'm afraid your father is very ill, *señorita*. We'll do everything we can to make him as comfortable as possible, but you should prepare yourself...'

Maria gave a small nod. It wasn't really a shock. She had known it already.

The doctor explained the nature of her father's illness. 'If he had come for treatment at the beginning, we could have done something for him. But that is no longer possible.' She turned to Raul. 'Are there people who should be notified? Can you help her with that?'

'I'll do everything necessary. Maria is in my care.'

'May I see Father now?'

'For a few minutes, yes. But he's had medication which has made him very drowsy. He may not know who you are.'

Very early the following morning, when the air was still cool, Raul drove Maria home by way of the track leading to the small settlement where Rosalba and her family and two other poor families lived.

In the night there had been heavy rain, but the four-wheel-drive vehicle was never in danger of being bogged down in the deep muddy ruts which by noon would be baked dry again.

Rosalba, unaware the Rawlingses had gone, burst into tears at the news that the American artist was never coming back. Maria, who still felt curiously numb, comforted her.

'But how will you live, *chica*?' the Mexican woman asked, when her sobs had subsided. 'You can't stay there by yourself. It wouldn't be safe . . . a girl like you on her own.'

'I'll look after Maria. You don't have to worry about her,' said Raul.

'Who is this man?' asked Rosalba.

'He's related to the English lady I told you about.'

'That doesn't mean he can be trusted. Men are men . . . whether they have bare feet or shoes that cost a lot of money,' said Rosalba, eyeing Raul's loafers.

'I'll be quite safe with him, Rosalba. He's going to help me pack up Father's paintings and the rest of our things. But I'll come back and see you . . . afterwards.'

'How long——?' Rosalba began.

But Raul stemmed her curiosity about the nature and duration of George Rawlings' illness, saying briskly, 'We have a lot to do and Maria wants to get back to the hospital as soon as possible, *señora*. Please excuse us.'

Maria had been worried that in the night a gust of wind might have blown over the easel, causing her father's last painting to be flung to the ground, coating the wet oils with sand. But it was where he had left it.

'It's a very fine portrait,' said Raul, looking at it.

'It's a wonderful painting,' she agreed, 'but not a likeness of me. She's an imaginary person . . . an idealisation. . .perhaps a memory of my mother with my hair.'

He was still studying the painting. 'Or the way you will be when you're grown up. . .a woman. How long will it take to dry?'

'A long time. But Father mostly uses the same size canvases. He has some special pins to fasten them face to face, with a small space between, so that they don't get smudged when he mails them to the man who sells his work.'

It took less than an hour to pack up their entire household and load it into the Range Rover. Maria would have left the hammocks and her clay cooking pots for whoever took over the hut. She knew Rosalba was right. She couldn't live here by herself. But Raul insisted she must take all her belongings.

On the drive back, once they were on the highway, the sun and fatigue made her fall asleep. She didn't wake up until they were back in Cancún.

'I'm going to drop you off at the clinic and then I'll have all this stuff put in storage,' said Raul. 'I'll be back as soon as I can.'

'But haven't you more important things to do than looking after me?'

He glanced at her but didn't answer until, a few minutes later, he parked in a space outside the clinic's main entrance. Then he switched off the engine and turned to her.

'Did you believe the things your father said about me the other day?'

Maria shook her head. 'He was ill...not himself. I couldn't argue with him.'

'There's a lot of truth in his indictment of developers as a breed. Shameful things have been and are still being done to beautiful areas. But there's no way to stop the tide of tourists who want to vacation in the sun. The time when a few privileged people could enjoy "unspoilt" places is over. In some ways I regret that as much as your father does. Because, like him, I'm one of the privileged,' he added sardonically. 'He's had where you lived to himself for a couple of decades. I have the means to spend my holidays in the parts of the world mass tourism hasn't reached yet.'

'I expect if you could have talked to him before he was ill, you could have made him see that,' she said quietly.

'Perhaps . . . perhaps not. I would think he and I have only one thing in common.'

Before she could ask what he meant, he went on, 'I'm not the villain he imagines. Nothing my companies have put up has been a blot on the landscape. However, that's a digression. You asked if I had more important things to do than help you to sort out your problems. Yes, I have other things to do today, but none more pressing than helping someone in trouble. Now go in and see your father and I'll attend to the matter of storing your gear. I'll be back as soon as that's organised.'

He leaned across her to unlatch the nearside door and push it open for her.

About an hour later they met in the corridor as Raul was stepping out of the lift and Maria was coming away from her father's private room.

'How is he?'

'They've given him something to make him sleep . . . and to dull the pain. We talked a bit. He's very weak. He's not angry any more . . . at being brought back, I mean. I—I think he's relieved that everything's out of his hands now.'

Raul nodded, his brows drawn together, his expression concerned and sympathetic. He said, 'While he's sleeping, I'm going to take you for a swim. It's important, in these situations, to get some fresh air and exercise, even if you don't feel like it.'

He took her lightly by the arm and pressed the button to recall the lift. 'I've brought a portable telephone. I'll leave the number with the receptionist downstairs and she'll be able to page us if for any reason you need to come back in a hurry.'

They had the lift to themselves. Trying to sound unemotional, Maria said, 'I saw the doctor again. She says it's only willpower that's kept Father going for so long. He's not going to hold out much longer...maybe a week...maybe less.' On the last words her voice cracked slightly.

Raul put his arm round her shoulders and pulled her close. 'He's had a pretty good life: painting...loving your mother...watching you growing up.'

The fraternal hug and his kind tone were too much for her. Her mouth trembled, her eyes filled with tears and she had to hide her face against his shoulder.

The loss of control didn't last long. Somehow she pulled herself together, fumbling for the handkerchief in her pocket and saying in an unsteady voice, 'I'm sorry. I'm not going to cry.'

'I don't mind if you do, sweetie.' He tilted her face up to his and gave her a kiss on the forehead.

At which point they reached the ground floor and the door slid open to reveal several people waiting to ascend.

Driving to the beach, which was some way from downtown Cancún where the clinic was located, Raul amplified what she already knew: that, only a few years before her parents had met, the fourteen-mile-long spit of sand and rock between the sea and the lagoon, now a long chain of hotels, had been deserted except for iguanas and other wildlife.

Maria listened and looked, but part of her mind was focused on what had happened in the lift. She knew his hug, his kiss and the endearment he had used had been merely the sort of response any man might have shown to a girl in tears, especially one he regarded as far less mature than most of her age group.

But even though she *was* deeply upset about her father and couldn't bear to think of what he had suffered, keeping his illness to himself, she knew that her pain and

grief were eased by being with Raul and that he, more
than either of her parents, could be—if he wished it—
the person she loved most of all. But of course he would
never wish for that. She was just someone in trouble
whom chance had thrown in his path but who had no
long-term place in his high-powered life.

He left the vehicle in the grounds of an hotel which
he concluded was part of his holdings. The beach was
reserved for the people staying there, but there weren't
many lying on the luxurious loungers.

'Shopping in the air-conditioned malls, probably,' said
Raul, when she remarked on this.

They swam, dried off in the sun, had a light salad
lunch with chilled mineral water, and returned to the
clinic where George Rawlings was still asleep.

During the afternoon he woke up and seemed pleased
to find her sitting beside him. When he began to talk
about his wife, Maria debated telling him about seeing
the house in Mérida where her mother had grown up
and about meeting his brother-in-law's wife. But she was
nervous of saying anything which might not please him.
How much his present calm was caused by the drugs
they were giving him, and how much by resigning himself
to the inevitable, was hard to tell.

Later, a nurse came to say that, if Señor Rawlings felt
up to it, Señor Dysart would like to speak to him
privately.

Remembering her father's half-demented maledic-
tions when he was prevented from swimming out to sea,
Maria wouldn't have been surprised if the request had
enraged him. But it didn't.

At the nurse's suggestion, she went with her to see
some especially magnificent flowers which had been de-
livered for a patient who was in the operating theatre.
Then the nurse took her to the day-room for conva-

lescent patients. There was no one there and they had
chat in Spanish until a buzzer attached to the other girl
uniform signalled that she was wanted.

Maria picked up a glossy magazine but she wasn't i
the mood to read beauty hints and study fashion phote
graphs. She put it back on the table and stood lookir
out of the window at the street below, wondering wha
Raul was saying to her father.

It was Raul himself who came to tell her their tête-à-tê
was at an end. But he didn't say what had been di
cussed and she hesitated to ask. He was in a hurry an
only stayed a few minutes before going off to some aj
pointment, saying he would see her later. When she r
turned to her father's room, the nurse had just give
him an injection and already he was half asleep.

'If I were you, I'd try to snatch an hour's slee
yourself,' said the nurse. 'I don't suppose you got muc
last night, did you?'

They were all being especially kind to her because c
what lay ahead, thought Maria, as she went up to th
top floor. And since there was no possibility of her fathe
recovering, she ought to confront the fact that very soo
she would be on her own with her living to earn and
large debt to repay. How was she going to do it?

She was woken by another nurse telling her she wa
wanted in Room 24.

'It's all right... you don't have to rush. He just wan
you there... to talk.'

Her father, when she joined him, came straight to th
point on his mind.

'Young Dysart was here a while back. This mornin
was it? They're pumping me full of dope... it makes m
confused. He says he wants to help you... send you t

stay with his old aunt. I said it wouldn't suit you, living in England. You're used to the sun. You wouldn't like grey skies and cold. Anyway I don't trust him. I'm not saying he means you harm, wants to seduce you. I don't think he has that in mind. But there's some- thing . . . something behind his suggestion.'

'So what did you tell him, Father?'

'That you're better off here. When I've gone you must write to my lawyers. You'll find the address with my papers in the envelope with my passport, your birth cer- tificate and our marriage lines. You've kept that by you, I hope.'

'Yes, it's upstairs in my room.'

He gave a satisfied nod. 'Everything you'll need is in there. But you won't get the money I've saved for you until you're twenty-one. I tied it up in a trust in case of accidents . . . and because, given the chance, you might be as wasteful with money as your mother was. She thought it grew on trees. If you're ever really up against it, the trustees'll let you have enough to tide you over. But I don't think you'll have any problem finding a job.'

'I'm sure I won't, Father. You mustn't worry about me. I'll be all right.'

'I hope so, Maria. Maybe I was wrong to keep you with me. Maybe . . .' His voice trailed off and he lapsed into another doze.

Three days later, he died in his sleep. The doctor in charge wanted to sedate Maria but she was reluctant to take pills and Raul supported her resistance. They were the only people at the funeral and afterwards he took her back to the hotel which was his current base in Mexico. It was not the one where they had been swimming every day. That, it turned out, belonged to Carolina's father.

The hotel owned by Raul's company was at the extreme southern end of the barrier island at Punta Nizuc, with access to a long white beach and also to the lagoon, Laguna Nichupté. Hidden from each other by beautifully landscaped sub-tropical gardens were a score of low colour-washed buildings, some with several bedrooms, some with one.

Maria was taken to a cottage with a double bedroom, a sitting-room and a spacious veranda decorated and furnished in a fresh-looking combination of cobalt-blue, white and coral.

Raul had told her to rest and they would meet for dinner at eight o'clock. In her sitting-room she found books, magazines, a basket of fruit and, in a concealed refrigerator, a selection of soft drinks and alcohol which, according to a discreet notice on the top of the cabinet, were provided with the compliments of the management. It was clearly a very expensive place to stay.

After she had unpacked, she put on her bikini and went in search of the beach. From it, the sea looked an even more beautiful colour than the view she was used to: jade changing to turquoise and then from blue to deep violet.

After her swim she went back to the cottage and showered. Then she wrapped herself in a long white cotton robe, also provided by the management and lay down on a white-cushioned day-bed to enjoy a luxurious book called *The Art of Mesoamerica* which had the hotel's book plate pasted inside the front cover.

She must have fallen asleep, for the next thing she knew was that the telephone on the table beside her was ringing.

'*Bueno.*'

'Good evening, Miss Rawlings.' A pleasant female voice answered in English with an American accent. 'M

Dysart asked me to remind you that he's expecting you for dinner in forty-five minutes. Someone will come to your cottage to show you the way.'

'Thank you.'

'Mr Dysart thought you would prefer to dine informally in private. Do you have everything you need?'

'Oh, yes, thank you.'

'Good. Please don't hesitate to ask if there's any way we can be of service to you. You'll find the house telephone directory on the writing table.' Whoever it was rang off.

Maria was relieved to know that they weren't going to eat in public in a restaurant where all the other women would be in fashionable resort clothes.

She put on the denim skirt and the peach-striped white shirt she had washed and pressed at night in the laundry-room at the clinic where, during the day, the patients' silk nightgowns and pyjamas were laundered by hand. When her hair was newly washed, a ribbon tended to slide off, so she fastened it back with an elastic band to hold the ribbon in place.

At two minutes to seven there was a light tap on her door. A young Mexican in an immaculate uniform with a name badge—'Arturo'—above the breast pocket had come to conduct her to Raul's quarters.

On the way she asked him how long he had worked at the hotel. He seemed surprised she spoke Spanish and said he had been there since it opened six months earlier.

Raul's cottage looked identical to hers. He was reading on the veranda.

'*Gracias, Arturo*. We'll have dinner in half an hour. What would you like to drink, Maria?'

She noticed the bottle of white wine in an ice bucket on the table beside his chair.

'May I have a little of your wine?'

'Of course. Would you like it diluted with soda?'

'Is that how you drink it?'

'No, but a lot of women like it that way. It's lighter in calories—which you don't have to worry about—and less alcoholic for someone who's driving. Try it. See what you think.'

When he had fixed her drink and they were sitting down, she said, 'Raul, this is a beautiful place and it's very kind of you to bring me here. But it's miles beyond my means. I don't know what they are yet. There's some money in trust for when I'm twenty-one but I shouldn't think it's very much and meanwhile I have to earn my living and try to pay back all the money you've already spent on my behalf. I'm afraid that may take quite a while, but I mean to start work the minute I can find a job. I'll start looking tomorrow.'

He lifted a quizzical eyebrow. 'That was quite a speech. Now it's my turn. In the first place we're not heavily booked at the moment so your cottage would be empty if you weren't in it. Secondly, you need to think about the future more carefully than you've had time for. This has all happened very suddenly. You need time to come to terms with it. I think you should take life easy for at least a week, maybe longer.'

'But I can't afford to do that. How can I sit back, doing nothing, when I have all these huge bills to pay...the clinic...the funeral expenses? I must owe you millions.'

'In pesos, yes. But it's not such a frightening amount in US dollars or sterling. Anyway, there are other ways of settling debts besides paying out money, you know. In this case there's a much easier way to cover your expenses ... one which doesn't involve taking some dead-end job which would bore you to death and pay peanuts.'

'There is?' she said, puzzled. 'What is it?'

CHAPTER NINE

'YOU can sell me your father's paintings,' said Raul. 'All the canvases he left. They're exactly what I want for the new hotel south of Playa. Rather than mailing them to the New York dealer he mentioned—who doesn't seem to have succeeded in whipping up much interest in them—let me take them off your hands. For what I'm prepared to pay, you can settle your bill at the clinic and the other expenses, with enough left over to pay for a course in the skills you'll need to get yourself a job with prospects.'

'Can they be worth as much as that?' she said doubtfully.

She had no idea what her father had been paid for his pictures, except that he'd often said sourly that dealers made more than artists.

'Even competent amateurs expect high prices these days,' said Raul. 'I don't suppose you've felt like looking at the paintings in your cottage, but in my opinion they're not as good as your father's work.'

In fact she had looked at the pictures and thought them decorative but not what her father would have classified as art. When Raul told her what they had cost she was astonished.

'There's a place downtown where girls go to learn keyboard skills,' he went on. 'How to type and use a computer for word-processing and so on. That's a basic qualification for almost any job you can name. I'm not sure how long the courses last. Not more than a month, I shouldn't think. But by the time you're through there, you'll have a better idea what you want to do with your life.'

Arturo reappeared pushing a rubber-wheeled trolley with silver covers protecting the dishes on it from the insects flying about the gardens. The absence of mosquitoes from the terrace was explained by gadgets plugged into electrical sockets.

The table was already laid with white napery, flowers and candles inside glass storm shades. When Arturo had lit the candles, Raul drew out a chair for her.

Their meal began with *sopa de aguacate*, a soup made from avocados served with hot sweet rolls.

'Tomorrow morning my secretary will find out about the course for you. I've left a space in my schedule to take you to one of the shopping malls. You're going to need some more clothes.'

'I feel I'm a terrible nuisance to you.'

'If you were, I should delegate someone else to look after you,' he said drily. 'I never do anything which bores me.'

After a pause, she said, 'Why is the hotel not full?'

'We're catering to a clientele who would normally turn up their noses at a resort like Cancún but who want to take breaks in the sun without going as far afield as, for example, the Bandaneira.'

'Where's that?'

'An island in a sub-group of the Moluccas which used to be called the Spice Islands. It's where I go for my holidays. But even today it takes a long time to get there and the climate is only good at certain seasons. From Europe, or East Coast America, it's not a destination which makes sense for a few days' break. Cancún is. At the beginning it attracted the rich *and* discriminating traveller. I'm hoping to draw them back. The way things are going, quite early in the twenty-first century, the

world is going to run out of beautiful unspoilt places in
the sun.'

When they had finished the soup, he uncovered a dish
of seafood salad and gave her a generous helping. For
the rest of the meal he talked about hotels and resorts
and she asked what she hoped were intelligent questions.

The sweet was a salad of fresh figs topped with nuts
and thick whipped cream and served with thin gingery
biscuits.

Afterwards, Raul said, 'Come into the sitting-room.
I'll show you a desktop computer which is what you'll
be learning to use.'

They sat side by side at a desk, with Maria directly in
front of the screen, while he showed her which buttons
to press to bring it to life and produce a list of the next
day's appointments, including '10.30 a.m: Take Maria
shopping'. But it wasn't going to last long. At noon he
had another engagement.

He said, 'If I've nothing better to do I can play chess
or solitaire.'

He gave her some more instructions. When she pressed
the wrong key, he put his hand over hers, took hold of
her forefinger as if she were a very young child, and
dabbed the pad of her finger on a sequence of keys which
not only produced a chessboard but moved several pieces
to different squares.

'Did you and your father play board games? I don't
remember seeing any.'

'We had some when I was small but they went in the
hurricane.'

She was sharply conscious of him leaning over her
shoulder, his hard cheek inches from hers. Then he
stretched his free arm round her, took her other hand
to control that forefinger as well and, a few moments

later, in the centre of the blank screen was her name in capital letters.

'See . . . you can make it bigger . . . or smaller . . . or rub it out and start again. These things are a lot of fun. You'll enjoy getting the hang of it.'

Then, to her disappointment, he put her fingers on keys which made everything disappear and then he let go of her hands and switched it off.

'Time you were in bed.'

Presently, brushing her hair, she wondered if he had known that being close to him made her heart pound and her pulses race and that was why he hadn't continued the lesson.

She was wearing the nightdress he had bought her. It was made of a cotton so fine it would have been transparent had it not been gathered into a band of smocking above her breasts. The neck and armholes were bound with yellow to match the thread used for the stitches on the smocking. She knew it must have been expensive. How had he known what size bra and briefs she wore and her waist and hip measurements for the skirt? Perhaps he had often bought clothes for women, or perhaps he had found a salesgirl who looked about the same size as herself.

Counting the hours until half-past ten tomorrow, she climbed into bed. For a little while she read, but the book didn't hold her attention. She put it aside, switched out the light and lay down to think about Raul and the new life stretching ahead of her.

The next day they went to a mall with over three hundred shops as well as cafés and restaurants. Maria was dazzled by the window displays.

When the time came to leave, she said, 'Could I stay here by myself and spend some more time looking around? I can come back by bus.'

Momentarily Raul looked doubtful. Then he said, 'All right. But don't let anyone chat you up. If they do, answer in Spanish. Make it clear you're not a tourist. I'll take your shopping back with me. Here's some money in case you see anything else you want. Have lunch here if you like, but be back by four.'

After he had gone, Maria spent more than an hour studying the window displays and looking at the racks of clothes inside the shops. At a food counter she bought a carton of yogurt topped with granola and sat on a bench by a fountain, enjoying the contrast between the crunchy topping and the rich, smooth taste of the chocolate yogurt.

She knew that if she could earn her living any way she wanted, she would like a job in the fashion industry. The way people dressed fascinated her. She could spend all day sitting watching the passing parade of tourists, analysing why some of them looked good and some looked terrible and, in the case of the latter, thinking how she would dress them.

But perhaps a career in fashion wasn't an option. More than anything she wanted to stay near Raul. Perhaps the way to do that was to make out she was interested in a job in the hotel or travel business.

When she continued her tour of the mall, she came to a gallery selling paintings and small sculptures. Curious to see what they cost, she had a look round. Admittedly the pictures were expensively framed but the prices confirmed what Raul had told her. Even second-rate art was expensive.

When she returned to the hotel and asked for her key at the desk, she was handed a folder with 'For the attention of Miss M Rawlings' attached to the cover.

Maria didn't look to see what it contained until she got back to the cottage where her shopping had been left on a chair on the veranda.

She changed into her swimsuit, filled a glass with iced water and sat down to open the folder.

Inside were receipted medical and funeral bills and a list of her father's paintings, identified by descriptions with suggested prices typed alongside. To her surprise the list included the portrait of herself which she wouldn't have thought would be there. She didn't like the idea of parting with it but perhaps she would have to. Another sheet of paper gave details and costs of learning secretarial skills. Raul's secretary had even found out what it would cost to lodge with a Mexican family in downtown Cancún. Finally came a sheet balancing the total amount offered for the pictures against outstanding and future expenses. If she accepted the prices offered, she would come out of the deal with her debts wiped off and a little money in hand to tide her over until she had her diploma from the business school and could start earning.

The day Maria finished her course, Raul took her out to supper and, while they were eating shrimp sautéd in olive oil with garlic and chilli peppers, told her he could get her a job on the excursions desk at the hotel owned by Carolina's father.

'I'd rather work in one of your hotels.'

'Maybe later on we'll have something suitable for you. This will be good experience. That's if you haven't thought of something else you'd rather do.'

She shook her head. She had made some enquiries on her own account: the sort of vocational training she would really like would involve going to Mexico City or America. Mexico City was already grossly overcrowded and in the United States she would be far away and friendless.

'What will I have to do?'

'Explain what tours are available to the visitors and liaise with the companies running the tours. You won't find it difficult. You'll be working shifts and there's a free minibus to take staff to and from the downtown area. You can go on living with the Vargas. You're still comfortable there?'

'Yes, it's fine.'

'And you're making friends?'

Maria nodded. The Varga family had a daughter about her own age who worked in one of the other big hotels. She had introduced her to people and Maria was making friends at her workplace. Several young men on the staff had tried to make a date with her, but she wasn't interested. The only man she wanted to see was Raul.

'I'm going to Europe for a couple of weeks,' he told her. 'If you have any problems while I'm away, tell my secretary.'

On her fifth day at the hotel, Maria was alone at the excursions desk when she looked up from studying a brochure to see Carolina approaching.

'Raul said he'd arranged for you to work here. I'm sorry about your father,' said the other girl. 'Mamá told me, if I saw you, to give you her sympathy.'

'Thank you.' It occurred to Maria that there was no longer anything to prevent her from telling Carolina who her mother had been. But not now, not while she was on duty.

'I don't come here much in the normal way, but I'm helping to organise a ball—a big affair for charity. So I'll be coming a lot. See you...' Carolina hurried away.

However although Maria often caught sight of her dashing through the lobby, sometimes she was busy attending to a guest and at other times Carolina was in too much of a rush to stop and talk.

Maria decided to postpone revealing herself as Isela's daughter. Perhaps it would be best to tell Raul first. She longed for him to come back. Even though she hadn't seen much of him recently, the knowledge that he was nearby made her feel more comfortable than when he was far away in Europe.

He came back unexpectedly, two days before he was scheduled to return.

The Varga family were out for the evening and she was lying in the hammock on their back porch, listening to music and day-dreaming, when suddenly Raul appeared round the corner of the house.

Taken by surprise, she could only stare at him in astonished delight. Then, as he stepped on to the porch, smiling at her, she tore off the headset and sprang out of the hammock, her face alight with joy.

'You're back!'

What happened next was spontaneous. He opened his arms to her, and she flung herself into them. But what began as a bear hug became, when she raised her face, the first proper kiss of her life.

She had often thought about being in Raul's arms and feeling his lips on hers. But her imagination hadn't prepared her for what it was really like. As he held her close to his tall strong body and took possession of her mouth, the emotions and sensations sweeping through her were as powerful and irresistible as the roaring winds and storming seas of a hurricane.

It seemed to go on forever and, when he raised his head and put her gently away from him, she felt sure he didn't want to and that it was an effort for him to resume his normal manner.

'Are you alone here?'

She nodded, gulping in breath to say, 'Did you ring the bell? I didn't hear. Everyone else is out this evening. Why are you back ahead of time?'

'I'd finished what I went to do. That side gate ought to be locked when you're on your own here. Anyone could walk through.'

'Come inside. Let me fix you a drink...or coffee...or whatever you'd like.'

'Thanks, but I only stopped by to say hello and check that it's all going to plan . . . that you like the job on the tour desk.'

'It's fine . . . for a starter,' she added. 'I wouldn't want to do it forever.'

'There was never any question of that. What are your hours tomorrow?'

When she told him she was on duty from eight until two, he said, 'We'll have lunch and maybe a swim. I'll go out the way I came in. Come and lock the gate after me.'

A few minutes later he was gone, leaving her wondering if it had been some kind of hallucination. But when she put her fingers to her lips she knew that she couldn't have imagined that rapturous kiss. Raul might not have meant to kiss her, and might think better of it afterwards. But it had happened. It had put their relationship on a new plane.

* * *

On the night of the big dinner dance, Maria was working the late shift and was still on duty when people in evening dress began to arrive.

Until the day before yesterday she had clung to the hope that Raul would include her among the guests at his table, even though she had nothing to wear for such a grand occasion and couldn't afford to buy a suitable dress.

Since his return from Europe they had lunched and swum several times. But he had never asked her out at night and his manner towards her was much the same as it had been before their embrace on the back porch. She was at a loss to understand how he could have kissed her in that hungry way and next day reverted to mere friendliness.

Some time after the tours desk should have closed, Carolina swept into the lobby, wearing a spectacular dress with a clinging silver top and floating white chiffon skirt. She came over to the desk.

'Like my dress?'

'It's beautiful,' said Maria.

'It's a Valentino,' Carolina told her, preening.

By this time Maria had looked at enough glossy magazines to recognise the name of one of the world's top designers.

Turning to watch the other girl's bare back as she swirled in the direction of the ballroom, Maria wondered if she would ever wear a dress like that.

'You should have gone home ten minutes ago.'

She came out of her reverie to find Raul standing by the desk. It was the first time she had seen him in evening dress. In a masculine way, he looked as breathtaking as his cousin.

'I wanted to see some of the dresses. Carolina's is wonderful.'

It struck her that they might have arrived together. Presumably Carolina, as one of the ball's organisers, had hurried ahead of him to check that everything was in order while he was parking the car. But surely there would be valet-parking tonight?

'She enjoys these affairs,' said Raul, his tone suggesting he didn't share her enthusiasm.

'Are her parents coming?' Maria still hadn't told him about her mother.

'They have another engagement tonight. But most of the people present will be in their age group. It will be extremely dull. If I hadn't been asked to keep an eye on Carolina, I shouldn't be here,' he said. 'If I'd known you were still in the building, I'd have kept the car and run you home. I'll get them to bring it back.'

'Oh, no, please don't bother.' Much as she wanted to be with him, she didn't wish to be a nuisance. 'I'll go on the next staff bus.'

At night, when there were fewer staff on duty, the shuttle service was less frequent but she didn't mind waiting.

At that point Carolina reappeared, urgently beckoning Raul from the far end of the ballroom corridor.

'Some minor crisis, I suppose. I'd better go and deal with it. Goodnight... Cinderella.'

With one of his sardonic smiles, he strode away, leaving her to regret that she hadn't jumped at his offer to run her home.

Two days later, in a special supplement, the local paper published four pages of photographs of the ball, including one of Raul and Carolina dancing together.

He hadn't been looking bored when the camera caught them, Maria thought, with a pang. Even before the photographs appeared, the staff grapevine had been

humming with speculation that he was courting tl
chairman of the board's daughter. She tried to dismi
the rumour as uninformed gossip but she couldn't shal
off the feeling that it might be true.

When her shift was over, instead of taking the b
downtown, she walked to the nearest shopping mall
look for an inexpensive gift for Señora Varga's birthd
at the weekend.

It was the mall where Raul had taken her shoppi
for clothes before she started her training course. As s
had before, she had a long browse in the dress shop
partly to take her mind off the dispiriting thought th
the kiss which had meant so much to her was never goi
to be repeated because, on Raul's side, it had been
misguided impulse he now regretted.

She was passing the picture gallery, on her way out
the mall, when a small canvas on a spotlit easel insi
the open doorway caught her eye. She had never se
the painting before but she knew it was one of l
father's even before she was close enough to see his devi
on it. Most of the pictures had prices on them, but tl
one didn't. 'How much is this picture?' she asked, wh
the dealer appeared from the back room. Perhaps, il
wasn't too costly, he would agree to let her buy it
instalments.

When he told her the price, at first she thought
was joking.

Sitting in Houston airport, waiting for the delayed c
parture of the flight to Amsterdam to be announce
Maria watched other travellers snacking at the fo
counters and browsing in the bookstore near where s
was sitting. She wondered if anyone else felt as unhap
as she did. How could you tell what was going on insi

people? How would anyone, looking at her, know that
her heart was breaking?

It had taken her three days to organise her getaway.
Three days of rage and pain at finding herself the dupe
of a man she had thought she could trust.

It was clear now why he had befriended her. He must
have known all along that her father was becoming recognised, that the paintings Raul had bought from her
for a song were worth a great deal of money.

Luckily a passport had not been a problem. When her
father had renewed his passport for his last trip to New
York, he had organised one for her.

'You never know what might come up. One day we
may want to leave here in a hurry,' he had said at the
time.

Now, for her, that day had come. This morning she
had left Mexico and would never go back. But to escape
had cost money. The only way she had been able to raise
it was by selling the portrait of her mother, the one
painting not on Raul's fraudulently priced bill of sale.

No doubt, had he known she had it, he would have
persuaded her to sell that for peanuts as well. Whereas
the dealer, when she revealed who she was and who the
girl in the painting was, had paid her more than enough
to cover her fare to Europe.

And to keep her for as long as it took to train for a
proper career so that for the rest of her life she need
never again be beholden to a man.

ENVOI

MARIA'S taxi joined the line of vehicles waiting to put down their passengers at the entrance to one of the world's most prestigious art galleries, the Prado, treasure house of paintings collected by the kings of Spain for five hundred years, including works by the great Spanish masters, Vélazquez, Goya, and El Greco.

Immediately in front of her taxi was an vintage Rolls Royce, ahead of that a new Ferrari. The distinguished the rich, the famous: everyone who was anyone was arriving for the reception to launch the first public exhibition of a large collection of paintings by the mysterious artist who had signed his work with a representation of a spider monkey, believed by the ancient Mayans to be the protective god of artists and scribes.

As her taxi drew nearer to the entrance, she saw she would have to run the gauntlet of Press photograph and TV cameras. But they didn't make her nervous. I was the imminent meeting with the man inside the building which made her inwardly tense.

She had already paid the driver by the time the door of the taxi was opened for her and she stepped out on to the special-occasions carpet, passing the barrage of cameras with the calm assurance of a woman who knew her appearance could not be faulted.

'Who's this?' she heard a male voice ask. The answer came from one of the women photo-journalists. 'It' Andrina...the designer. But she's not on the guest list.

Inside the building people were being directed to special cloakrooms set up for the occasion. Maria sur rendered the elegant black cashmere shawl, bound with silk and fastened by an antique silver cloak clasp, which concealed the upper part of her dress to an attendant.

The fact that she had no invitation wasn't noticeable at this stage. Not many of the woman shedding their wraps had come on their own and their escorts would have their cards.

The attendant collecting the invitations was at the top of an impressive staircase. In the background were two other men, in evening dress, whose discreet surveillance missed nothing.

Just before she reached the attendant, Maria stepped out of the line and said quietly to one of these men, 'Good evening. My name is——'

To her astonishment, he said, 'Good evening, Miss Rawlings. Please go in.' He touched the attendant on the shoulder and said in a low voice, 'This lady doesn't need a card.'

How did he know who she was? How did he know her real name?

Baffled, she accepted a glossy catalogue from another attendant and passed through the archway leading into the huge room where her father's paintings were displayed. It was not the first time she had seen them since leaving Mexico. In London and also in Paris, examples of his work had been sold by the fine arts auction houses and she had been to views and, later, read the reports of the prices they had fetched.

Even seeing them one at a time always gave her a strange sensation. Now to walk into a room where more than fifty of his best works were displayed was an unnerving experience.

Waiters were circulating with trays of drinks and titbits. Maria took a glass of sparkling wine which looked like champagne but was more likely the finest Spanish *cava*. She declined the selection of vol-au-vents and other savoury mouthfuls offered to her.

Everywhere she looked were vivid reminders of the country where she had grown up and the eccentric genius who had been the centre of her world until that unforgettable morning, long ago, when another man had entered her life and left an equally indelible imprint on her heart and mind.

Had this been an ordinary exhibition, she would have begun to move slowly round the room, studying the paintings one by one. Tonight that was impossible. She was too keyed up. Indeed at this stage hardly anyone was looking at the paintings. For the moment they were busy socialising: greeting people they knew, performing introductions, the women eyeing each other's clothes.

The only painting which was receiving attention was one in the centre of the room. From where she was standing Maria could see no more than a corner of the frame and glimpses of the wine-coloured silk rope of a cordon preventing people from crowding too close to the easel supporting the frame.

Curious to see which of her father's works had been selected for this place of honour, she moved closer.

As some people standing in front of it moved aside, she was startled to see her own face looking back at her. Suddenly it was clear why the man on duty at the entrance had recognised her.

Instinctively she turned away before anyone else should notice the likeness between the suntanned girl in white in the painting and the untanned blonde guest in black whose hair was coiled into a chignon, not loose down her back, but who was clearly the same person.

Opening the catalogue, the better to hide her face while she recovered from this second shock, Maria found the portrait reproduced as a frontispiece. It was captioned,

'Portrait of the artist's daughter, Maria, aged nineteen. See notes on page fifteen.'

She was turning the pages when someone said, 'Good evening, Miss Rawlings.'

She turned to find a man she had never seen before at her elbow.

'Mr Dysart has been told you are here. He'd like to see you before the official opening. Would you come with me, please.'

This was a turn of events she hadn't foreseen. Somehow it had never occurred to her that Raul would include her portrait in the exhibition, or that the likeness would be so much more striking now she was older.

'Very well.'

'This way. Let me dispose of that for you.' He took her untouched glass of wine and gave it to a waiter.

They left the room by a side door giving into a passage hung with Old Master drawings. Her escort held open a fire door and, a few yards further on, showed her into a small room dominated by a huge Biblical painting. She had braced herself to find Raul there, but the room was empty.

'Mr Dysart will join you in a moment.' The man withdrew.

Maria hadn't bargained for meeting Raul in private. But perhaps it was better this way. She felt herself starting to tremble and took some more deep, steadying breaths. At the moment she had the whip-hand and she mustn't lose it. If she showed the least sign of weakness, he would quickly recover the dominance he had once had.

The door opened. She turned, her face a mask of hauteur.

For a moment he stood in the doorway and, because he was wearing a white dinner-jacket, she had the curious illusion that time had gone into reverse, like a rewinding video, and at any second they would be back in Mexico on the night of the charity ball.

Then he stepped into the room, closing the door quietly behind him, and she saw that he wasn't the man she remembered. She wasn't the girl she had been, and the years had changed him as well. His hair was as thick as before but premature flecks of grey were visible at his temples and his face, still darkly tanned, was thinner than she remembered.

'Good evening, Raul,' she said coolly. 'Is there some special reason why you wished to see me? If not, I would rather be looking at my father's paintings. It's purely by chance that I happen to be in Madrid this evening.' This was true. If she hadn't seen the piece in *The Times*, she wouldn't have known about the exhibition. 'I'm leaving first thing in the morning.'

In recent years she had seen a number of men fighting to control their tempers, although not because she had provoked them. Raul's eyes didn't bulge nor did his face turn purple. But his anger showed in the sudden hard knots of muscle at the angle of his jaw and the compression of his lips.

'Damn right there's a special reason!' he said, without raising his voice. 'When you ran off, you caused a number of people a great deal of needless anxiety.'

'Really? I can't imagine who. Certainly not you! You must have been delighted to see the last of me.'

'We'll leave my reactions out of it for the moment. You worried Aunt Iris out of her wits when she found out. She'd grown very fond of you. You worried Conrad because he was fond of her. Perhaps you don't remember Conrad. He was old and you only knew him for a short time. None of us meant much to you. That's obvious.'

'On the contrary, if I'd known your aunt's address, I'd have kept in touch with her... as long as it didn't involve me in any more contact with you.'

She had never forgotten the strange steely grey of his eyes, but the blaze in them now was something new to her. 'What is that supposed to mean?' he demanded.

'You could hardly expect me to feel kindly towards you once I found out you'd cheated me. In my innocence, what you paid for the paintings you bought from me seemed a huge sum at the time. But it was only a fraction of their real worth. I didn't know that, but you did.'

To her surprise he showed no sign of discomfiture. 'When did you find that out?'

'Soon after you duped me. It's the reason I left. I did think about facing you with it but then I decided not to. It seemed better to cut my losses and forget I'd ever known you. Which I did. As no doubt you forgot about me... until I turned up tonight and you felt yourself threatened.'

'Threatened?' The characteristic lift of the eyebrow hadn't changed. 'What are you talking about?'

'It wouldn't be difficult to expose the mean trick you played on me. I still have the receipt for the paintings, or rather my lawyer has it. If I chose to tell the Press...' She left the sentence unfinished. 'I should feel uneasy if I were in your shoes.'

His eyes narrowed. 'What do you want from me? Money?'

She gave him a scornful look. 'You would jump to that conclusion. No, I'm not a blackmailer, Raul. I don't want your money. I wouldn't touch it with a bargepole. It galls me to think I was ever under an obligation to you. Is Miss Dysart still alive?'

Clearly he found the question irrelevant, but he said curtly, 'Yes, but that's not her name now. She's Mrs Huntingdon. She and Conrad decided to marry soon after you disappeared. You would have been asked to their wedding but you couldn't be traced. Are you married?'

She shook her head. 'I've been too busy carving out a career. As your aunt's still alive and I shouldn't like to distress her, I'll leave things as they are. But you know and I know that, morally, some of those paintings out there—the nucleus of your collection—don't really belong to you. You got them by means that no honourable person would stoop to. I hope you can live with that, Raul. I know I couldn't.'

While she was speaking his expression had changed. His eyes were no longer angry. The grim line of his mouth had softened.

He said, 'The years since you went haven't been a good time for me, but not for that reason. We'll talk this out later, Maria. In a moment I'll have to go and take part in the opening.'

As he said it, the door opened and the man who had brought her here put his head in. 'It's almost time, Mr Dysart.'

'I'm coming, Stephen. Look after Miss Rawlings, will you? I haven't finished with her. I hold you responsible for seeing that she stays in the building.'

'Yes, sir.'

Raul strode out of the room.

'I don't know how he expects you to stop me if I choose to leave,' Maria said, fuming.

'I shall lose my job if I don't,' the man called Stephen told her, with a wry smile. 'Mr Dysart expects his orders to be carried out to the letter. If not——' He gave an expressive shrug.

'Don't worry. I won't give you the slip. Having come, I want to see the exhibition. Some of the paintings I've seen before. Others are new to me.'

'There's a small gallery above the entrance to the exhibition-room. You can watch the opening from there if you'd rather be incognito,' he told her.

'Much rather. I had no idea the portrait of me was going to be on show.'

They reached the gallery by a narrow flight of stairs which led even higher, perhaps giving access to the roof of the building. In the gallery were three or four chairs. Sitting down, Maria could see over the balustrade without being seen by the fashionable throng below.

It was a long time since she had seen so many beautifully coiffed heads and haute couture dresses. This being Spain, many people were smoking and the aroma of cigars, pomades and colognes took her back to the night of the engagement party in Mérida.

As the most important guests began to appear on the dais, to be met by ripples of applause and bobs and bows from the people nearest to them, she wondered if Carolina would have changed much. Probably by now she and Raul had at least two children, but it seemed unlikely that his cousin would have let her figure go like Mexican women of the poorer classes.

Raul was the last to appear, but there was no one with him. Perhaps Carolina was pregnant and had chosen not to come, although she would have to be very close to the expected birth date to miss an occasion like this, thought Maria.

'Where is Mr Dysart's wife?' she murmured to her companion.

He looked puzzled. 'Mr Dysart isn't married, Miss Rawlings.'

'D'you mean he's divorced now?'

'To my knowledge he's never been married.'

What had gone wrong? she wondered.

On the dais a man moved to the lectern with the microphone attached to it and waited for the hum of murmured conversation to die down. 'Your Excellencies, ladies and gentlemen . . .

As he began to speak, Maria remembered what she had been about to read when Stephen interrupted her. She opened the catalogue to check the number of the page with the notes relating to her portrait.

Looking at it again, she remembered the last time she'd seen it, the day Raul had helped her to pack their belongings. Then her glance flicked across to the facing page, the title page of the catalogue. As she was about to turn it, her own name sprang to her eye from the small print below the large letters at the top.

All the paintings are the property of the Maria Rawlings Endowment which has its headquarters in Mérida, Yucatán. After being exhibited in Europe, the collection will be housed in a nineteenth-century mansion in Mérida, formerly owned by the family of the artist's Mexican wife.

For some moments Maria felt stunned. The man beside her was listening intently to the introductory speech. When it finished and he joined in the clapping, she put her hand on his arm.

'What does this mean?' tapping the paragraph with her finger. 'There was nothing about this in *The Times*.'

'No, it wasn't mentioned in the first Press releases. It's going to be announced in a minute. It's a trust set up by Mr Dysart to establish and maintain a private art gallery.'

'But why was it given my name instead of my father's?'

'Because that's the way Mr Dysart wanted it. I wasn't on his staff when the Endowment was set up. I've only been with him four years. It was already——' he broke off as another speaker stepped forward, the American ambassador.

Maria listened in a daze to the ambassador's expressions of pleasure at the increasing fame of an artist whose career, he said, had many parallels with that of another American, Georgia O'Keeffe. She had found her finest inspiration in the landscape of New Mexico while George Rawlings had found his in the seascape of Mexico's Caribbean coast.

His speech was followed by a reminder that the artist's mother had been English from the British ambassador. Then a speech by the chairman of the Endowment's board of trustees was announced.

Compared with the three previous speakers, all men in late middle age and all rather overweight, Raul looked strikingly lean and virile. From the gallery, the flecks in his hair were invisible and Maria felt she must have imagined that he looked curiously drawn. Now, acknowledging the applause with his charming smile, he looked as compellingly attractive as her memory of him.

After the formal preamble, he said, 'About fifteen years ago, in New York, I saw a painting which caught my imagination. The gallery was small, the price of the picture was low. I bought it. There was no signature, only a squiggle of paint which I wouldn't have recognised for what it was if I hadn't spent time in Mexico. Not long after that, a more astute dealer recognised the artist's worth and drew him to the attention of the critics. Late in life he began to be fashionable. But he continued to live in seclusion with his daughter in whose name the Endowment was founded.'

He paused to glance round the room and Maria wondered if he was looking for her.

'The portrait of Maria Rawlings is one of the finest paintings in this travelling exhibition,' Raul continued. 'And George Rawlings transmitted his artistic gift to his daughter who, since his death seven years ago, has established herself as a designer. Many of you will know her by her professional name—Andrina.'

A murmur of surprise ran through his audience and Maria wondered how and when he had found that out.

The rest of his speech concerned her father and the quest to trace all his paintings and, where possible, acquire them for the gallery in Mérida.

'We had better go back to the ante-room,' said Stephen, as the people on the dais began to step down and mingle with the other guests. 'Mr Dysart may want you to join him.'

'Nothing would induce me to join him in that mêlée,' she said decisively.

Her thoughts were already in turmoil. To be obliged to be gracious to a throng of people she had never set eyes on before would be beyond endurance.

Stephen looked rather shocked. 'Hardly a mêlée, Miss Rawlings.'

'Perhaps not, but I still don't want to meet them. Mr Dysart's wishes may be a categorical imperative to you... but not to me. If he wants to see me, I'll give you my telephone number. I'd also like to see the paintings in peace and quiet. Perhaps he could arrange for me to come to the Prado before it opens to the public tomorrow. I'm sure that's not beyond his powers.'

By now they were going down the stairs with Stephen ahead of her. He turned to look over his shoulder. 'Yes, certainly... but I think he'll want to see you tonight.'

In fact Raul was already in the passage leading to the ante-room.

'I can't imagine that you want to meet a pack of strangers and I'm not in the mood for them either,' he said briskly. 'Stephen, you can deputise for me. I've already apologised to both ambassadors and said my presence is urgently needed elsewhere. Come along, Maria. You and I have a lot to catch up on. We'll slip out the back way.'

Taking her arm, he led her back through the fire door but then turned down a different passage to where a security guard was on duty.

'This lady is feeling unwell,' he explained in Spanish. 'She's staying at the Ritz Hotel. We want to leave by a door which isn't under Press surveillance.'

'Do you want a car called, *señor*?'

'No, no, it's only a stone's throw. The fresh air will do her good.'

'This way, please.'

A few minutes later a less imposing door was being unlocked for them. While she was inside the building, Maria had forgotten how cold it was outside.

'My wrap!' she exclaimed.

'We can retrieve it later. There's not far to go.' Raul stripped off his dinner-jacket and wrapped it round her.

Fortunately the heels of her shoes weren't so high that she couldn't hurry. Very soon they were in the warmth of his hotel where she shrugged off his coat and gave it back to him, noticing as she did so the muscular breadth of his shoulders under the silk of his dress shirt.

The porter had his key ready for him. Going up in the lift, she said, 'When did you find out my working name?'

'Between leaving you with Stephen and joining the VIPs on the dais. One of my PR people told me. There'd already been an enquiry from someone in the Press contingent who'd seen you arriving and recognised Andrina and Rawlings' daughter as one and the same. I don't know why none of my PR staff made the connection... or how you managed to elude my efforts to trace you. Do you realise that the whole point of taking this exhibition on tour is to flush you out of hiding?'

'I wasn't in hiding, Raul. I wasn't aware that you wanted to find me.'

'There were a lot of things you weren't aware of,' he said, looking down at her. 'One of them being that I was in love with you.'

'I—I thought you were going to marry Carolina.'

'You were wrong,' he said curtly. 'I was waiting for you to grow up. It would have been easy to sweep you off your feet then. But I wanted you to feel the same way I did. At that stage, you had no idea how beautiful you were or what the world had to offer you. The only other man you'd met was that young Dane, Eriksen.'

She was surprised he remembered him, until, as the lift doors opened, Raul said, 'It was he who let me know you were all right... but not until after you'd left Denmark.'

Startled, she said, 'Chris wrote to you? But he promised he wouldn't.'

'He was in love with you too. Was that something else you chose not to recognise?' he asked sarcastically, as they walked along a thickly carpeted corridor with elaborate arrangements of flowers on gilded consoles.

'He was then. He's married now...very happily. What did he tell you?'

'That you were safe and well. Nothing more. I went to Copenhagen to see him. He was reluctant to meet and I couldn't get anything out of him. He refused to say where you'd gone or why you'd left Cancún. But at least I knew you were safe and had him to turn to.'

Raul unlocked at door and stood back for her to pass into a lobby opening into a luxurious sitting-room. Again Maria was reminded of Mérida and the suite they had shared with his great-aunt. It seemed a lifetime ago.

'I had Eriksen watched for a time, hoping he might lead me to you,' he said. 'But he didn't leave Denmark and you didn't go back there. I concluded you had merely been using him.'

'That's not true,' she flared. 'At the beginning he was the only person I could turn to. I didn't know then that Father had left me some money... quite a lot of money. I wrote to his lawyers in New York to inform them he'd died, as he'd told me to, but it was some time before all the formalities were completed and I found I wasn't as destitute as I thought. Chris always knew how I felt about you. The only thing I didn't tell him was what you had done... what I thought you had done.'

'You really believed I would rob you?' Raul asked coldly.

'What else was I to think? The evidence was there in black and white... the amount you'd paid for the paintings and what I was told they were really worth. Why *did* you do that, Raul?'

'To keep you under my eye. As soon I could take a break from the Playa project—all our operations in Mexico needed my close supervision to keep them on schedule—I planned to take you to England where you could have enrolled in a fine arts course or something of that sort. But you jumped the gun. No doubt, from your point of view, it's worked out better than my plan.'

'Perhaps. At least I have the satisfaction of having built my career without anyone pulling strings.' Her gaze wandered round the room. 'Even if you've never heard of Andrina, most designer-conscious women have. In my professional persona, I could and would have stayed

here at the Ritz, if I hadn't wanted to avoid the possi
bility of meeting you in the lobby. That would have
spoiled my plan.'

'Which was?'

Maria looked him in the eyes. 'I was going to expose
you... publicly. And then I looked at the catalogue and
realised that I'd narrowly missed making a total fool o
myself.'

'You must have built up a deep hate to be ready to
go to those lengths.'

'Wouldn't you... if someone you'd loved seemed to
have taken a contemptible advantage of you? I wa
nineteen, Raul. My confidence in myself was as fragile
as a bubble. I couldn't believe someone like you would
prefer me to Carolina. I find it hard to believe now. Why
would a man who had everything want the naïve young
thing I was then?'

'Perhaps because he could recognise all the innate
qualities which have made you the woman you are today.

'You don't know what kind of woman I am now. It'
been a long time... we're strangers.'

He came to where she was standing and took her chin
in his hand. 'There hasn't been a day when I haven'
thought about you... worried about you... wanted you
back. Do you remember the *cenote*... the Sacred Wel
at Chichén Itza?'

His touch made her tremble inside. 'Of course.'

'I'd been there several times... but always before i
was an ancient ceremony, too far in the past to hav
much reality for me. That day it was different. I though
of you being thrown in and——' His lips twisted in
wry smile '—it was like having my heart torn out.'

And then she was in his arms and they were holdin
each other as if these were their last moments togethe
before another even more terrible separation.

Clinging to him, feeling his arms round her, Maria was afraid that it might be some crazy dream devised by her subconscious and that at any moment she would wake up.

'Oh, Raul...it's been so long...so lonely,' she murmured brokenly, her face pressed against his shoulder.

'I know. But it's over now. You won't escape me again.'

He crushed her to him, his arms like steel hoops binding her painfully tight until he suddenly realised she wasn't built to withstand that kind of pressure and relaxed it.

'Maria...look at me.'

She lifted her face, blinking away tears of relief and happiness.

'Can you forgive me for thinking such vile things about you?'

'I could forgive you anything.' He bent his head and kissed her, gently at first and then, as she responded, with increasing passion.

RUGGED. SEXY. HEROIC.

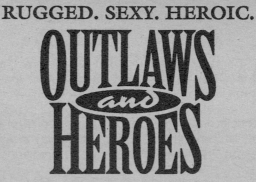

OUTLAWS and HEROES

Stony Carlton—A lone wolf determined never to be tied down.

Gabriel Taylor—Accused and found guilty by small-town gossip.

Clay Barker—At Revenge Unlimited, he *is* the law.

JOAN JOHNSTON, DALLAS SCHULZE and MALLORY RUSH, three of romance fiction's biggest names, have created three unforgettable men—modern heroes who have the courage to fight for what is right....

OUTLAWS AND HEROES—available in September wherever Harlequin books are sold.

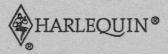

HARLEQUIN®

THREE BESTSELLING AUTHORS

HEATHER GRAHAM POZZESSERE
THERESA MICHAELS
MERLINE LOVELACE

bring you

THREE HEROES THAT DREAMS ARE MADE OF!

The Highwayman—He knew the honorable thing was to send his captive home, but how could he let the beautiful Lady Kate return to the arms of another man?

The Warrior—Raised to protect his tribe, the fierce Apache warrior had little room in his heart until the gentle Angie showed him the power and strength of love.

The Knight—His years as a mercenary had taught him many skills, but would winning the hand of a spirited young widow prove to be his greatest challenge?

Don't miss these **UNFORGETTABLE RENEGADES!**

Available in August wherever Harlequin books are sold.

FLYAWAY VACATION SWEEPSTAKES!

This month's destination:

Glamorous LAS VEGAS!

Are you the lucky person who will win a free trip to Las Vegas? Think how much fun it would be to visit world-famous casinos... to see star-studded shows...to enjoy round-the-clock action in the city that never sleeps!

The facing page contains two Official Entry Coupons, as does each of the other books you received this shipment. Complete and return all the entry coupons— **the more times you enter, the better your chances of winning!**

Then keep your fingers crossed, because you'll find out by August 15, 1995 if you're the winner! If you are, here's what you'll get:

- Round-trip airfare for two to exciting Las Vegas!
- 4 days/3 nights at a fabulous first-class hotel!
- $500.00 pocket money for meals and entertainment!

Remember: The more times you enter, the better your chances of winning!*

*NO PURCHASE OR OBLIGATION TO CONTINUE BEING A SUBSCRIBER NECESSARY TO ENTER. SEE REVERSE SIDE OF ANY ENTRY COUPON FOR ALTERNATIVE MEANS OF ENTRY.

VLV KAL

FLYAWAY VACATION
SWEEPSTAKES
OFFICIAL ENTRY COUPON

This entry must be received by: JULY 30, 1995
This month's winner will be notified by: AUGUST 15, 1995
Trip must be taken between: SEPTEMBER 30, 1995-SEPTEMBER 30, 1996

YES, I want to win a vacation for two in Las Vegas. I understand the prize includes round-trip airfare, first-class hotel and $500.00 spending money. Please let me know if I'm the winner!

Name_____

Address _____ Apt. _____

City   State/Prov.   Zip/Postal Code

Account #_____

Return entry with invoice in reply envelope.

© 1995 HARLEQUIN ENTERPRISES LTD.   **CLV KAL**

FLYAWAY VACATION
SWEEPSTAKES
OFFICIAL ENTRY COUPON

This entry must be received by: JULY 30, 1995
This month's winner will be notified by: AUGUST 15, 1995
Trip must be taken between: SEPTEMBER 30, 1995-SEPTEMBER 30, 1996

YES, I want to win a vacation for two in Las Vegas. I understand the prize includes round-trip airfare, first-class hotel and $500.00 spending money. Please let me know if I'm the winner!

Name_____

Address _____ Apt. _____

City   State/Prov.   Zip/Postal Code

Account #_____

Return entry with invoice in reply envelope.

© 1995 HARLEQUIN ENTERPRISES LTD.   **CLV KAL**